THE CURFEW

THE CURFEW

Jesse Ball

VINTAGE CONTEMPORARIES

Vintage Books • A Division of Random House, Inc. • New York

A VINTAGE CONTEMPORARIES ORIGINAL, JUNE 2011

Library of Congress Cataloging-in-Publication Data
Ball, Jesse, 1978–
The curfew : a novel / by Jesse Ball.
p. cm.
"A Vintage Contemporaries Original."
ISBN 978-0-307-73985-8
1. Fathers and daughters—Fiction. I. Title.
PS3602.A596C87 2011
813'.6—dc22
2011001509

Book design by Rebecca Aidlin

www.vintagebooks.com

Printed in the United States of America
10 9 8 7 6 5 4 3

For Alda Aegisdottir

We are born in this cemetery, but must not despair.

—Piet Soron, 1847

PART 1

∧

There was a great deal of shouting and then a shot. The window was wide open, for the weather was often quite fine and delicate during late summers in the city of C. Yes, the window was wide open and so the noise of the shot was loud, almost as though it had been fired in the room itself, as though one of the two people in the room had decided to shoot a gun into the body of the other.

This was not the case, however. And because no one in the room itself had been shot, the man, William Drysdale, twenty-nine, once-violinist, at present, epitaphorist, and his daughter, Molly, eight, schoolchild, slept on.

Those were their methods of employment. Daily, Drysdale went about to appointments while Molly went to school and was told repeatedly to repeat things. She could not, and didn't.

In the street beyond the window, it was very shady and pleasant. An old woman was bleeding, hunched over a bench. Two men were standing fifty feet away, one holding a gun. Some ten feet from the bench, a man was lying underneath the wheels of a truck, which seemed to have injured him, perhaps irreparably. The driver was kneeling and saying something. He stood up and waved to the two men. The one with the pistol was putting it away. Another, smaller truck arrived for the bodies. The man who had had the pistol, but no longer showed it— he was directing people to go away. People were going away.

One minute after the gunshot, the street was empty. This was often the case. I shall introduce this city to you as a city of empty streets—empty only when something occurred, momentarily empty and soon full again, but empty nonetheless.

I shall introduce this city and its occupants as a series of objects whose relationship cannot be told with any certainty. Though violence may connect them, though pity, compassion, hope may marry one thing to another, still all that is in process cannot be judged, and that which has passed has gone beyond judgment, which leaves us again, with lives and belongings, places, shuttling here and there, hapless, benighted, discordant.

^

It was a school day and so, after a while, the two in the room began to stir. Molly woke first, and dressed herself. She was an able child, although mute.

—We will get something on the way, said William.

Molly nodded to herself. She stood by her folding pallet in the corner of the room and held up before her the two dresses that were hers. One was blue and the other yellow. Which to wear?

And then they were in line at the bakery, and she had on the yellow, which matched her somewhat torn yellow dancing slippers, although she did not dance. She did not have a bag with books because it was not that sort of school.

—Two of those, said William. And one of those.

—Do you want one now? he asked.

Molly signed, *Not yet.

Well, what sort of school was it, then? It was one of the schools where you sat in rows on benches and the teachers told you what to think. You recited things and wrote things repeatedly. You read from books that were held on little chains to the tables. Examinations were given, and often sticks were employed to instill discipline. There was a little area of dirt where they could play at lunchtime. Play was encouraged, as was snitching.

*Here we are, said Molly.

—Goodbye! said William, and caught her up for a moment.

She ran inside the building. Other children pushed past him as he stood there watching after.

—Drysdale, did you hear?

A coarse man of advancing years was there with wife. One might confuse either for a banker.

—Latreau's dead. Shot this morning.

—The old woman? For what?

—Pushed someone in front of a bus.

—I heard it was a truck, said the wife. She thought the man was a cop, so she pushed him in front of a truck. But they caught her before she could get away.

—I'm sorry to hear that, said William absently. I truly am.

His lips hardly moved.

William walked away without looking at either of them. He hadn't looked at them once the whole time. If one had been watching, one might even have thought that the couple had just been speaking to each other. William was that cautious.

∧

The town was called a town, but it was a city. This is a convention of the very largest cities. It had districts: old districts, new districts, poor districts, trading districts, guard districts. There had been a jail once, but now there was no need for a jail. The system was much too efficient for that. Punishments were either greater or they did not occur at all. An ordinary nation, full of ordinary citizens, their concerns, difficulties, cruelties, injustices, had gone to sleep one night and woken the next morning to find in the place of the old government an invisible state, with its own concerns, difficulties, cruelties, injustices. Everything was strictly controlled and maintained, so much so that it was possible, within certain bounds, to pretend that nothing had changed at all.

Who had overthrown it? Why? Such things weren't clear at all, just as it wasn't entirely clear that anything had been overthrown. It was as if a curtain had been drawn and one could see to that curtain but not beyond. One remembered that the world had been different, and not long ago. But how? This was the question that nagged at those who could not avoid asking questions.

^

The nothing that had changed at all was really beyond bearing. Houses and buildings were full of desperate people who deeply misunderstood their desperation. This was due to artful explanation on the part of the government. It is impossible to tell, many said out of the corners of their mouths, if the ministry is thinking well of us—if they are acting on our behalf. Yet still there were acorns falling from trees, fish breaking the surfaces of ponds, etc. In a long life, said many an old man, this is but one more thing. Yet there were others who were young and knew nothing about the helplessness of life's condition. Did they glow with light? They did, but of course, it could not be seen. And all the while, the grinding of bones like machinery, and the light step of tightrope walkers out beyond the windows.

But recently, only recently, those who could not bear to be governed in this way had taken steps. It was impossible to say exactly what had altered, but clashes between the two sides were now common, and the people of the city had grown used to the finding of bodies without explanation.

Such explanations, of course, may only be offered later, when one side has won.

∧

William headed to his first appointment. He pictured himself as he would be seen, a man in a long tweed coat, with a stick under his arm, with a bowler hat and a pair of sturdy black shoes. Then, he inserted himself into that image, as an actor would.

In such made and imagined clothing, he arrived.

—Mrs. Monroe is in the garden.

A servant led him down a tiled passage. The tiles had pastoral scenes: cows, gypsies, birds of different sorts, wattle buildings, haystacks. No two of them were the same. This had a disquieting effect. You would obviously never have time to sit and look at all of them, even were it possible, and so it gave an elusive impression. William wouldn't like to be forced to give an opinion about it.

The passage opened onto a shady porch that overlooked a stand of trees and a lawn. The whole thing was walled in. An elderly woman with straight gray hair and a mauve housecoat was seated on a wicker divan.

—You are the mason?

—No, I work for him. I am helpful in finding the best way of putting things, a way that everyone can be happy with. The epitaph, you understand.

—It isn't particularly important who is happy, other than myself. I'm the one buying the gravestone. I'm the one who knows the wishes of my husband, who'll lie underneath it.

The woman coughed violently, covering her mouth with a pillow from the divan.

William began patiently:

—There is the cemetery to be thought of: they don't permit just anything. And, of course, the state has been known to remove memorials of one sort or another. We would not want for such a thing to happen.

—I see.

William sat in a chair that the servant provided. He took a small leather notebook out of his pocket, and a pencil. While the woman was watching him, he brought out a knife with a very small blade and sharpened the pencil. Then he opened the notebook to a new page, wrote on it:

MONROE +

—Well, he said, what do you think, to begin with?

—Paul Sargent Monroe, said the woman. Died before his time.

—That's it?

—That's it.

—He was quite old, however, that's true, no?

The woman gave him a very serious look.

—Ninety-two.

—Well, are you sure you want it to say, Died before his time, on the gravestone? I don't mean to say that we can't do that, because, of course, we can, if you like. It just seems a bit, well, just not exactly right.

—I see what you mean, said the woman.

They thought for a minute. Finally, she broke the silence.

—Well, we could change the date.

—The date?

—Have it say: Paul Sargent Monroe. Died before his time. And change the birth date to twenty-five years ago.

William shuffled his feet.

—I suppose that's possible, but . . .

—You see, said the woman, when people are in a cemetery, and they see the grave of a young man, they stop
and feel sadness. If someone lived for ninety-two years,
the throng passes on by. They don't stop for even a
moment. I want to be sure of, well . . .

—I see what you mean.

A few more minutes passed. William looked occasionally
down at his notebook. He had written there:

MONROE +

---

and then a line, and then:

PAUL SARGENT MONROE

Died before his time.

He took a deep breath.

—Well, he said. If you're going to do it that way, maybe it's better to have him die as a child. It could be that he was six when he died, and the inscription could read, Paul Sargent Monroe, Friend of cats. It would evoke his personality a bit, and certainly people would pause there.

A sort of ragged quiet was broken by another fit of coughing.

Happy tears were in the woman's eyes.

—I see why they send you, she said. You're right, just exactly right. That's just what we'll do. After all, it doesn't matter what the truth of it was, does it? It's just to have people stop, and be quiet for a moment. Maybe it's late in the afternoon and they're on their way some-where, to a restaurant. They stopped at the cemetery briefly, and then they pass his grave, and, oh, now they'll stop a moment. Now they will.

She took his hand in both of hers.

—I do wish you could have met Paul. You would have liked him, and he would have liked you.

—I believe it, said William. I feel sure of that.

He got to his feet, closed his notebook, put it in his pocket. The pencil he snapped in half and put in the other pocket. He used each pencil exactly once, for one epitaph. He brought as many pencils as there were appointments, and he sharpened each one as he began.

—Goodbye, he said. We will send you a proof of what the stone will look like, and you can initial it.

—Thank you so much. Goodbye.

He stood and headed for the tile passage.

She called after him:

—And do you know what? He *was* a friend of cats. He really was. He really was.

He looked back at the woman, but she was now occupied with something in her lap, a box of some sort and its contents. She did not look up.

^

Next he came to a gate. A man he knew, Oscar, was there. He stood next to Oscar for a minute.

A crowd of schoolchildren went through Oscar's gate, shepherded by a matron in a severe smock.

Oscar laughed.

—When I was a kid, you know, I had a tremendous fear of horses. I felt very uncomfortable about their shape, and I was horrified that I was completely alone in this. Once, I read about a war a long time ago where thousands and thousands of horses were killed by machine-gun fire. I felt very comfortable about that. There was a black and white photograph in the book of a field of dead men and dead horses. The perspective of the book was that the horses were not to be blamed.

—But you felt differently.

—I felt differently.

An old man drove up in a car with a rattling engine. His car was licensed to a different city. It was stuffed with belongings. He looked very tired, and slowed down very little. He came very near to running someone over as his car emerged on the other side.

The man who had been nearly run over had fallen. He got to his feet and came through the gate.

—That man has something in his pocket that looks like a gun but is probably a piece of fruit. If he should be shot for a piece of fruit it would be very unfortunate.

—How do you think they know, the secret police, who else is or is not secret police? For instance, this man with the fruit—if it was a gun, how would they know to shoot or not shoot him?

—But it is a piece of fruit.

—And if he was shot for it?

—It is a good idea to eat fruit when you buy it and not carry it around, my friend. Anyway—it is far nicer to stand nearby a fruit stand and eat the fruit than to carry it home and put it on a counter.

—I disagree.

—With this, William Drysdale, you cannot disagree. It is the way of things. I have never seen you carrying fruit in your pocket.

—Because I am afraid of being shot.

—Well, we will all be shot for something. I have a gold nose that I bought once, do you know that? This was many years ago. Apparently people used to lose their noses from syphilis and then they would sometimes have gold noses.

—This is a very clumsy way of changing the subject, Oscar. There is not even a single gold nose in sight to act as a segue.

—Well, I thought I saw one. A man is coming now with a very shiny nose. He should be careful, with such a shiny nose. It could mean trouble for him.

^

On then to the next appointment. This was a row house where houses were all slate-roofed. Every window in the street had bars across it. At that moment the sky was tremendously blue. For the first time in a long while, William looked down and saw his hands. If you have had this experience, you'll know just what I mean.

He knocked on the door.

After a minute, he could hear footsteps. The door opened. A man and woman were standing there. They appeared to be husband and wife.

—I'm from the mason.

—Yes, we've been expecting you. Won't you come in?

They brought him through the dark low-slung house to the back, where a long narrow window with many clear square panes afforded some measure of light. It was a room of three chairs.

—This is where we thought we'd talk, said the woman.

—We thought it would be all right in here, added the man.

—That's fine, said William.

He sat in one of the chairs and took his notebook out. This he set on one knee. From his pocket he took an unsharpened pencil.

Then, out with the knife, and he began his sharpening.

He looked at the couple.

—The stone is for your daughter, I believe?

—Yes.

—She was, nine years old?

—Just nine.

—I'm sorry to hear it.

The couple looked then the one at the other.

William continued,

—You see, I have a daughter who is nine.

The woman flinched as if hit.

—Be careful with her, she said. Our Lisa seemed indestructible, fearless, invincible. But all it takes, all it takes is . . .

Her voice was drowned out by her own crying. Her husband put his arms around her.

—It was a roof slate that did it. Right here in the street. The wind blew it. She had gone out to play and an hour passed, two hours, three. We just thought she was with a friend, or, well, I don't know what we thought. Anyway, Joan went out front to see if Lisa was coming, and . . .

The room was empty except for the three chairs. There weren't any pictures, there wasn't a table, just bare walls and this long narrow window of exactly square panes. Each of the panes was square, William observed for the third time. He looked at them in turn, yes, all square, leaded glass.

The man was trying to continue, but it took him a little while.

—You see, she was just there, right in front of the house, on the ground. The rest of her was fine, it was her head that, well, it had sailed down, the slate, and, the wind must have really sent it. I guess it didn't make any noise as it came.

—I'm sorry, said William. It is a terrible thing.

—We want it to mean something, said the woman. We thought about it, and this is a place where it can be made to mean something, don't you think?

—I'm sure of it.

—We thought it would begin with the name, that's how they go, and then,

—So . . . Lisa Epstein. Did you want the name in capital letters?

—Yes, clear large lettering.

The man broke in,

—Perhaps, perhaps, She was walking in the street by our house, and it was almost evening.

—We thought of it, you know, several different ways. What do you think?

They looked at him then, very intently.

—I think, perhaps, well, let's look at it. How old, exactly?

—Nine years, twenty-four days.

He leaned over his little book.

Lisa Epstein.

She was walking in the street by our house,
and it was almost evening.

He took a deep breath and leaned back in the chair. He
closed his eyes, opened them, looked at it again. He
looked up and around the room, avoiding the eyes of the
couple. Wherever he tried to look, his eyes were drawn
to this narrow ledge of light, this eighteen-paned window. It was the room's nature, and the three chairs were
the expression of that nature. That wasn't right, though,
not exactly. There weren't three chairs. There were two
chairs, and then one that wouldn't be used. He wondered
if he was sitting in the chair that the girl used to sit in. It
could even be that the room had changed completely,
that the girl had never entered the room under these con-
ditions.

—Do you sit here often?

—We sit here in the evening.

He looked again at his book. Lisa Epstein. Lisa Epstein.

He went to a new page.

LISA EPSTEIN
9 years, 24 days.

In the street by our house, it was almost evening.

He showed it to them.

∧

A thing that develops in a child—that which must occur particularly, precisely, if great success is to be had in some field—is not the prefiguring of that excellence, no! It is not the ability to produce great things of a lesser sort leading upwards like a ladder. It is rather a vague listlessness that infects other matters, leaving the single matter clear.

But then, of course, there is the matter of RIDDLES which must be learned by hand or with great violence of tutelage. Why, I shouldn't mind being beaten with a stick if it meant I could solve all riddles without exception. Yes, William had been whipped until he had the whole Exeter book by heart. No wonder then, the rise of this second profession, epitaphorist.

There is a theory that the sun is made up of thousands of suns arranged in a war each against the others. It is a discredited theory, but it has never been disproven.

∧

He took an oblique route to the next place, and passed through several alleys, which were themselves connected to other alleys. Here, the backs of things could be seen, unrepaired, unconstructed, unrepentant. Still, one was not unwatched. Faces could be seen beneath ruined stair-wells and from the mouths of makeshift tents.

Down the first side-alley he saw a man running, and several men in pursuit. The man who was running ran in an odd way, the way one runs only if one's hands are tied. Of those who chased him, one had a catch pole with a wire on the end. It ducked towards the first man's head again and again, but he kept ahead and shot around a corner. The others raced on, relentlessly, and all were gone from sight.

How could the government's people know one another? The simple answer, and the truth of it, as far as William could tell, is they did not. Government men were often caught by other government men and taken into the huge death cell rumored to be in the city center (no one had ever seen it). Once captured, the truth or falsehood of their claims could be decided. It was a small difficulty that permitted them to go at large without uniforms, operating with impunity.

The next place was a business. It was a butcher's shop, a huge one. As he entered, he emerged into a place for standing before a long counter, perhaps ninety feet in length. Behind it stood ten or fifteen men dressed in long white aprons. The counter was wood on top with glass, and William had never in his life seen so much meat in one place.

As it is described it seems very still, but in fact, there were dozens of customers in line, and the men behind the counter were strenuously engaged in great business of cutting, slicing, wrapping, tying. They dodged past one another, and past innumerable blades and cleavers with acrobatic motions.

William bypassed the line, and a young man, also in an apron, approached him immediately.

—You'll need to wait there.

—I'm not here to buy anything.

—In that case, you certainly need to stand over there. If you just want to look around, come by at some hour when we're less busy.

—No, no, I'm here on business. Mr. Denton asked me to come.

—Denton? Well, why didn't you say so? Come with me.

The boy gave the line a stern look before turning away, to make sure everyone stayed exactly where they were.

—Over here.

He walked William down to the end of the shop, where a small stair led to a door.

—I go no farther, said the boy. It had better have been true what you said. Denton doesn't like soliciting.

He hurried away back down the stairs.

William then opened the door and went into one of the tidiest, most comfortable rooms he had ever been lucky enough to encounter.

There was one very fine leather chair directly in front of a large window that overlooked the shop. All around were bookshelves, full of books of every kind, although he could see that many pertained to butchery and to animal anatomy. A drafting table was against one wall. The whole room was lit by candles, perhaps sixty of them. Before the drafting table, which was meant to be used standing, stood a large man of formidable characteristic.

—Mr. Denton?

—You are from the mason, I assume.

—I am that.

—Sit over there, please. I will fetch a stool.

Denton opened a closet and removed a three-legged stool. He placed it beside the sumptuous leather chair.

—Sit down, he said again.

He was about fifty, with a weathered face and deeply brown, almost black eyes. He wore the same aproned outfit as the men below, but his was the definitive version.

William sat. Out of his pocket, the notebook. He began to sharpen a new pencil.

—That's a fine little knife, said Denton. Marzol?

—It is, said William.

—I knew it. Those take quite an edge, quite an edge. I won't lie to you, I have more than a few of them myself, although substantially larger. The only meat you'll cut with a knife like that is a man's throat.

William blinked, and tried not to flinch as the man sat on the stool and rested one burly arm on the armrest of the leather chair.

—So, this is how it is. My father's dead. He started this business. Made it what it is now. People will always need someone to do their butchering, that's what he used to say. Do you know he could butcher a cow in any of thirteen different ways? How do you write an epitaph for a man like that?

—Robert Denton, that's how we'll start, said William matter-of-factly.

—Robert Denton, that's right.

—So, any thoughts? Some people like to put something simple, in remembrance, others like to really make the person's presence felt. Sometimes the epitaph is an inside joke—something only the deceased would understand.

—I do have something like that, said Denton.

The door opened, and a man nearly as big as Denton stepped into the room.

—Wilson fell under an ox, and his leg's bent.

—Well, call over Hal Sanderson. He'll put it right. As for the ox, is it dead?

—It was dead. He pulled it off a beam and it dropped on him.

—I see. Well, that's how it is.

—Right.

The door shut.

—I've got something, said Denton. He often said he could skin a pig with the lights off. He even said he did it once, although I never saw it.

—That's good, said William. That's really good.

He wrote:

ROBERT DENTON

who could skin a pig *in the dark.*

—I like it, said Denton.

William went to the door.

The two shook hands.

—They made me think, down there, you might be a hard man to deal with, said William.

—Don't fool yourself, said Denton. I'm a mean bastard. You just caught me at a tender moment.

—Well, I'll get to work on this.

Denton nodded.

^

He was out on the street again. A man jostled his elbow.
It was . . . William looked away.

—Will? the man said.

Will did not stop walking.

—It's you, isn't it? he said again, catching up. Well, of
course it is. I haven't seen you in quite a while. It's, actually, it's very fortunate to meet like this.

Will continued on, and didn't look at the man.

—Will, I need to speak to you. Do you hear me?

He grabbed William's arm and pulled him around.

—Sit down with me, there, in that cafe?

—We mustn't be seen. Come after five minutes.

∧

—Do you see what I mean? It's crucial. It's everyone's place—everyone is in a position to act, at some point.

A man with a long moustache and a military-style coat was muttering into his soup. This man had come in five minutes after William. He had sat at a table near the front, but then knocked over a bottle of wine and asked for another table. He had been moved to the table next to William. This man was William's friend. William had not spoken to him in four years.

—I don't know what you mean, said William.

—Even you, said his friend, even you must have heard of it.

—It seems just like the purges. I'm not interested.

—It's not the same thing, not at all. That's them killing us. This is us killing them.

His friend's moustache moved ornamentally as he spoke in precise, deliberate sentences. It was as if the conversation had been rehearsed.

—Did you rehearse this conversation?

—And if I did?

—It would make me feel like you thought it was important.

—It is important.

—Then did you rehearse it?

—Perhaps.

—If you did, then who did you have as me?

—Whalen.

—No? Whalen? Is he still around?

—Of course.

—It doesn't matter. I have Molly to think of.

—Come tonight, please. The address is on that sheet. It's necessary. Louisa would have wanted you to. You know that.

William held his hand close to his face. He didn't say anything.

His friend's face, turned away from him, addressing an empty table off to the right, became somehow slightly cruel.

—If nothing else would get through to you, I will say this last, that I intended to save for a place of greater privacy. We have had news of Louisa and what happened to her.

William flinched and involuntarily his eyes fixed on this man who seemed to have appeared out of nowhere in sudden frightening focus.

His friend stood, and William watched him walk through a door behind which lay the lavatory. He did not return. This was a typical method of leaving a restaurant. If William was the sort to meet people at restaurants, he might well have employed that same technique, but as it happens, he was not.

^

He sat there, with the crumpled sheet in his hands. An address. He had not gone to someone's address in a long time. He didn't even know how to begin to do such a thing. And this, if he went there at eight, it would mean returning after curfew, a danger in and of itself—such a danger as he had not taken on in years.

Any danger to himself seemed to be a danger to Molly. But wasn't that just an excuse for cowardice?

And Louisa, if he could learn something of Louisa. He felt again as he had on the day she vanished, and the feeling of waiting, restlessly waiting, was fresh upon him, but tinged now with a dire, hopeless grief. He shook his head as if to cast off a weight.

The day before, Molly had handed Will a piece of paper. That piece of paper did not have an address on it. That piece of paper had said:

———————

I am an elephant today. I will need to have lots of room and also a bowl of water on the floor.

———————

William had taken the largest mixing bowl from the cupboard, filled it with water, and set it on the floor.

He had found some cardboard also and wrote on it:

ELEPHANTS ONLY.

This he had put near the porcelain bowl.

Was he becoming a coward?

∧

And if he was, then what was the worst of it—

that there is nothing worse than to be the daughter of a
coward! or so it seems to the coward.

^

William ate the rest of his lunch in silence. He put what he had learned in a box and he shut that box. To do otherwise would be to give signs that he had learned something, some new information, and such behavior—indicative of new information—is what alerts those who seek after traitors. He could not even consider having learned that which he had learned, which after all was practically nothing. Just an idea, a hope of an idea. Away with it for now.

He had ordered pea soup with sourdough bread. The pea soup was very peppery and that pleased him, but he was not happy with the spoon he had been given, which was rather shallow for soup eating. He began to dip the bread in the soup, and in between bread dipping he would take spoonfuls. He had measured it out so that when he had the final taste of soup, it would be accompanied by the last bite of bread. However, the spoon's shallowness made the whole proposition laborious in the extreme.

Unbidden, the thought of Gerard came again. What could he know?

He should not go. He wouldn't. It was out of the question. But of course, of course, he must go.

Yes, there are times when something is asked of us, and we find we must do it. There is no calculation involved, no measure of the necessity of the thing itself, the action that must be performed. There is simply an acknowledgment that we will do the thing in question, and then the thing is done, often at considerable personal cost.

What goes into these decisions? What tiny factors, invisible, in the jutting edges of personality and circumstance, contribute to this inevitability?

The restaurant was quiet. A couple, sitting across from him, was whispering. On the table in front of them sat a decanter full of water. He could see the woman's face through the decanter, but distorted. It appeared to him that she was crying, but then she moved in her chair, and he saw that she was not.

The waiters were standing together by the door to the kitchen, and they also were conferring quietly.

There was a little breeze, like the movement of a finger, and it came and went.

I was a great violinist, thought William. What does that mean?

He returned the same way. He could see the gate from a ways off, and through the open door, the double chair. The back of Oscar's head was visible. The light came through the open door, making an oblong area that placed the chair in a sort of spotlight.

There is a space in the playing of a virtuoso piece where the violinist must cease to think about the music, must cease thinking of fingerings, even of hands and violins, where the sound itself must be manipulated directly. At such times even to remember that one has hands, that one is *playing,* is disastrous.

William had stood many times before an audience, playing such pieces, and it was in this way that he sought to control the very passage of his life, deftly and without forethought, yet precisely and with enormous care. Part of it was to allow what was enormous, what was profound, without limiting it.

And if he should be forced to give up music? He had been. And if he should be forced to lose his wife? He had lost her.

He came closer now, and saw the gate, and the wall, and the gatehouse. The whole thing was simply to have people be watched. To delineate areas in which people felt watched and areas in which they didn't. It was one more surface on top of the other surfaces.

He paused there by the wall to consider his position.

An hour passed, and the sun weakened by the gate. In the long afternoon, people of every kind passed by.

A young woman with a very short skirt and a thin blouse came out of a building in the distance. Because she was so beautiful, he saw her from far away, and for the same reason, he watched her as she came all down the road and through the gate. She wore her beauty very carelessly, and she left no one unaffected.

She was on the verge of dropping some of the things she was carrying, and in fact did drop them, at various points in her approach to the gate. But each time, someone came and picked up whatever it was, and handed it to her, and she accepted it, and appeared surprised each time that something should fall from her hand.

When she came closer, William saw that one side of her face was horribly deformed. That was why she had been dropping things—she had to walk in a very special way in order to keep one side of her face hidden from the crowd on the sidewalk.

To the next appointment he went hurriedly. He did not hurry out of worry that he would be late, but because it was the appearance of virtuous citizens—hurrying.

He found the house near the rail station. It was a large building with many apartments. Outside there was a huge signboard. It said,

VERACITY IS UNAVOIDABLE

in thirty-foot-high letters. Underneath in small letters, it said, Government Ministry 6. William had often wondered where the Government Ministries were situated. Their locations were not publicly known. The system was virtually invisible.

He was waved on by the doorman, who wore a remarkable gold-stitched uniform. There was no elevator. Instead—a grand staircase usually reserved for descending.

Many fine lamps here and there. Apartment 3L. He knocked.

A girl in a dressing gown opened the door.

—Come in, Mr. Drysdale.

William nodded.

—We are aware of you, she said, and walked ahead of him to the living room.

There, an elderly couple, her parents, sat amidst lavish furnishings. She sat, and he did the same.

The elderly couple inspected him quietly.

—He was her husband, you see.

—Our son-in-law.

—Died in the night, two weeks ago.

—Two weeks, three days, said the girl.

—There is no body. The body was taken. He has been . . .

—Accused, said the girl. It is unlikely that we will bury him. Nonetheless, we would like a stone.

—For her to visit, said the father.

—We will go with her, of course, said the mother.

William took out his notebook. He took out a pencil and his knife. He sharpened the pencil.

At the top of the page he wrote:

?

He looked up.

—The name?

—Jacob Lansher.

—Have you considered what you would like the stone to say?

Meanwhile, he wrote on the page:

Jacob Lansher.

The state of the room really was remarkable. It was full of contraband things. It was, in short, the house of a government minister, or seemed so. And yet, the disappearance of the husband.

—He was a writer, said the girl.

—Not exactly, said her father.

—He was.

—Dora, said her mother sharply. You agreed.

Dora looked away.

The mother handed William a piece of paper. It said:

———————————

Jacob Lansher

Dutiful Husband, Devoted Son.

———————————

—We've agreed upon this.

—I refuse, said Dora. He would have hated that.

—He made his decision, said the father.

Dora was on her feet.

—You know more than you'll say.

—If I do, said her father, then you're lucky.

The girl stormed out of the room. William was left staring at the parents.

—We make no apologies for her, said the mother. She is a grown woman.

—He was a dissenter, said the father. He couldn't change. He was always thinking of how things were. It was the end of him.

William wrote on the page:

———————————

Jacob Lansher

Dutiful Husband, Devoted Son.

———————————

He closed the notebook. He set the pencil carefully in his pocket.

—It will be as you say.

—Thank you. Have them send the bill around.

He stood up, nodded to them, and went back along the hallway to the door. He opened it and closed it behind him. He proceeded to the staircase and stood

for one

minute,

then

another.

^

The door to the apartment opened. The girl came out. She joined him by the staircase.

William took the pencil from his pocket and opened the notebook.

—There will be two stones, he said. The first will be as they say. You determine the second. You cannot go to it, unless you are sure you are not followed. Do you understand?

Dora murmured yes.

William wrote on a new page:

Jacob Lansher

---

then beneath it

John ACBLASER

---

then

John Cable Ras
John Carables
John Sarcable

—Sarcable, he said.

—That's good.

William leaned against the rail and squinted his eyes. He wrote on the page.

—That's good, said the girl again. John Sarcable. Elsewhere and beloved.

She smiled.

—One thing, and thank you. White marble, and leave room for his wife, when she dies.

He broke the pencil in half and put the pieces in his pocket.

—Goodbye.

∧

William stopped on the final step, and thought for a moment of the stairs he had been thrown down as a child. It was an accident. A woman thought that he was her son in the darkness of the building and, in great anger, had hurled him headlong. The actual boy was there too, but did not get thrown.

William had broken both his hands, and they had healed in a rather odd way. It was later thought by aficionados that this breaking of his hands was an advantage in his violin playing, and there was an ill-advised spate of hand breaking that went on until it was seen the accident could not be successfully replicated.

The woman was imprisoned and drowned herself in a washbasin. William never heard what happened to the son, but he often felt that if his life were a book, the boy would intercede at some point to take some terrible blow meant for William.

On then to his final appointment. For this he went out of the city gates and a little ways down to a waterfront and harbor that stretched there. He passed a woman who was putting up posters that read, MY HUSBAND HAS DISAPPEARED AND I MUST FIND HIM, with a photograph of a middle-aged man standing in a doorway wearing a prerevolutionary suit. William did not meet her eyes as he passed.

By the last pier, there was a shack with a sign that read:

FISH if you WANT THEM.

He knocked on the door of the shack, which made an awful racket.

—Coming!

A young man came to the door.

—Yes?

—I'm from the mason.

—The mason?

—Yes, about the gravestone.

—Ah, the mason . . . yes, well. I would ask you to come in, but I imagine you wouldn't like it at all in here. I mean, I live here and I don't like it at all. We'd be better to just sit over there on that bench.

He pointed to a bench on a hill overlooking the harbor.

—Sure enough.

The young man shook his hand.

—So, you might think this a bit strange, but the tombstone I want is actually for myself.

William nodded.

—Won't be a problem. Are you intending to . . . fill it soon?

—Fill it?

The young man blushed.

—Of course not! I just, well, I will explain it.

They walked up the hill to the bench and sat down. The young man was wearing fisherman's waxed clothing that was quite dirty. He himself had the sheen of good health and a thin but shining face. He seemed a very happy fellow indeed.

—I have a theory, the young man said, that a person should prepare his or her tombstone at the happiest moment of life. I am right now, for no reason at all, as happy as a person could possibly be, and so I decided, yesterday, to prepare my tombstone. I want nothing of sadness in it. Just rejoicing, you see?

—There is one danger, said William.

—What's that?

—Well, although you feel now that this is the happiest you can be, what would happen if, in the years to come, you became happier still?

—I would simply make another gravestone! I have done it three times already.

—What did the others say?

—Oh, I can't tell you that. I don't want them to influence this one.

—Understood. All right, well, what sort of epitaph are you interested in? Do you want it to be a general address, a private message, a warning, what do you think?

—A warning?

—Well, some people favor something like, Watch Out. Or, Hell Rears Its Head.

The young man burst out in peals of laughter.

—Certainly nothing like that. Perhaps something about my shack. I've just gotten it, you know.

William took out his pencil and sharpened it. He opened his notebook. So, your name?

—Stan Milgram.

He wrote:

Stan Milgram

Dweller in shacks

—That's not quite right, said Stan. It's just one shack. And anyway, maybe the shack isn't that important. I just, well, the whole thing came from Death Poems—where some people would prepare a death poem, so that they would know for sure it would turn out well. But then I want it to reflect these brilliant days I have come to now.

—What do you do?

—Fishing, and I sit around there in the shack and read.

—What if it gave a catalog of your day? Tell me about your day, what happened?

Stan told him in detail about the day's events.

—All right, then.

William turned to a new page.

STAN MILGRAM

4 AM, rose, already dressed, and set out for the boat.

5 AM, out on the water to the shoals.

6 AM, net after net of powerfully squirming fish.

& 7, 8, the same.

9 AM, returned to the docks.

10, 11, read Moore's Urn Burial;
ate an onion, cheese, brown bread.

12, closed eyes for a moment.

4, woke and met with the epitaphorist,
and set down this record.

—I would like to see a gravestone like that, said Stan proudly.

—I also, said William.

—The writing will have to be rather small.

—Not in itself a large obstacle.

—It isn't, is it?

—Nope.

—Let's settle it, then. Thank you. How did you come by this work, anyway?

—I was always good with puzzles, and I have memorized the complete works of five poets which I can recite on command. Four years ago, when I could no longer do the work that I did before, I saw an advertisement in the paper. It read, *Position requiring: ingenuity, restraint, quiet manner, odd hours, impeccable judgment, and eloquence. Unworthy candidates unwelcome.* I was the only one to apply.

—That sort of thing, said the young man. That sort of thing I understand effortlessly. It seems the way things should work.

William smiled and shook his hand, broke the pencil in half, tucked away his notebook, and set out back towards the gates.

THE STONEMASON

had a few small houses by the cemetery, with a yard around and between them. The whole thing was walled in, as you can imagine, with a high stone wall. The grass was short and yellow and patchy. The trees were old and august.

Smoke rose from the chimney of one of the houses. To that one William went.

—Mercer, he said, a good day's work done.

—I'd expect no less.

Mercer, a man of about fifty years with a ruddy face and thick clever hands, was grinding a piece of granite. He stopped his work and went with William into the next room, where the fireplace was. They sat.

—Let's see it.

William handed him the notebook.

He read slowly through it, nodding sometimes, sniffing, narrowing his eyes.

—I see, he said.

He set the notebook in his lap.

—Can the girl be trusted? This could be trouble, and for nothing.

—Not for nothing.

—No, not for nothing. But can she?

—I believe so.

—Good work, then. These will be attended to. And how is Molly today?

—Seemed happy.

—You know, the rhyme she made me, I say it every day. The paper she wrote it on is gone. But I remember it.

—When was that?

—Last winter. She was here the whole day while you went around.

—I remember.

—She came to me, and I was chiseling away, in the midst of it, you know, and she had a scrap of paper. It said Mercer on it, and underneath, to be said on mornings, and under that the thing.

—I asked you what it was and you wouldn't say, and I asked her, and she wouldn't either.

Mercer grinned.

—It's a thing like that. Not to be bandied about.

He set to coughing again. Finally he settled.

—On the way here this morning, I saw a woman killed.

One of the gnarled hands was gripping the other.

William waited.

—I was under the walking bridge on Seventh. There was a shout and then she came down, hit not twenty feet in front of me. Then right there where she fell from, a face looking down.

—Did she look like a cop?

—What does a cop look like, these days?

—So, the body was there, and you walked past it.

—Looked to see if she was dead, and she was. Twice over. People don't fall like cats, you know. Even cats don't always fall like cats. Have you ever seen it? When a cat does something it *knows* a cat shouldn't have done? There's nothing like the embarrassment of cats.

He laughed.

There was a little stove, and William made a pot of tea. The two men sat there while the water boiled, and then Mercer made the tea.

—I do prefer good tea leaves, he said. In a fine tin.

—If I saw any, I'd bring it. These days it can't be bought.

There was a book there, of old tombstone designs. William leafed through it.

There were many there he liked, and he showed them to Mercer. These were also ones that Mercer liked. They sat there, then, together, liking them.

The mason picked up his chisel. It was a splendid tool, an old tool, extremely heavy. William was very fond of Mercer and of all the things that Mercer owned. There are a few people one meets whom one can approve of entirely, and such was he.

—You keep that chisel sharp.

—I like to think I could cut the heart out of a sheep without it knowing. Just the tap of a hammer, and a slight twist.

—But you've always been fond of sheep.

—And am, and am. I'm speaking of the chisel, you understand.

There was the humming of an airplane overhead, but neither man looked up or made as if to notice.

—Tomorrow's list is by the door, said Mercer finally.

He handed William the notebook. William tore the pages out of it and set them down. White marble for the last, he said. And leave room, she says.

—We're all planning our own death these days.

—Tomorrow, then.

^

At six o'clock, he picked up Molly and they had a glass of lemonade by the lake.

*Can we rent a boat and go out to the island?

*No.

*But what about tomorrow? Can we tomorrow?

*No.

Molly played in the enormous gnarled oaks that had stood in the park for more than a century. Their limbs were long and bowed and many. Nearly every one could be climbed easily, and Molly had climbed nearly every one.

There was a man selling newspapers. William bought a newspaper, but did not read it. It looked bad to avoid the newspaper; one bought it, but one didn't actually have to read it.

He had not performed violin in over four years. There were no musical performances anymore. There were no performances of any kind. There was a new ideal, and one could sit in an audience and listen to people talk about the new ideal, but that was the extent of it.

Much of his life in the past years was a matter of making it so that things could not get worse. He tried to, through a series of habits, insulate and barricade the life that he and Molly lived, so that it could not be invaded or altered.

He had done this in a series of ways. First, he bought an apartment in an area of town that was known to be very quiet. He established a policy of having no friends, none at all. He ceased to speak to the friends he had had before. He got a job as a mason's assistant. He and Molly lived cheaply, and wore old clothes. They did simple things together quietly. They learned sign language together, for Molly couldn't speak. He taught her to read by himself, and he taught her mathematics by himself. He taught her to use an abacus. He taught her everything that she would need to know in school, and he did this when she was five and six, before she went to school. Therefore, school would have no difficulties for her, and her muteness would not be a problem.

Every night he and Molly ate supper at a little cafe some distance from their home. Molly sometimes played with a boy who lived in the same building, and while she was doing that, William would sit at the window and read, or play through a volume of old chess games with a small wooden chess set. He loved the games of Tchigorin and also of Spielmann. Neither one had been the greatest

chess player of his time, but their games were full of sac-
rifices and wild, inventive play. For such things, William
would say to himself, for such things . . .

There was no difference between any one day and any
other. The weekend had been abolished. It had been a
sick way of going about things, that was the idea, a sort
of illness that had led to widespread moral decay. Many
of the ways that things had been gone about were weak,
and had to be changed.

*There was a new teacher in school today.

—A woman?

*A man.

—Old?

*Rather not.

—Handsome?

Molly made a face.

—That bad?

*He wrote a book about history. The history of the coun-
try.

—And how did that go over?

*Jim spat on him and then they took Jim in the next room for a while.

—So, Jim, he's a history lover?

Molly did the thing that she did when she would have laughed but wasn't laughing.

William laughed as well.

*He just spits on teachers.

A ripple came and then subsided in the lake, as though a fish had surfaced, but none did.

—There is a game, William said, where you try to throw a stone high up in the air and have it make just that noise, the noise of a fish at the water's surface. It is not easy to do.

William threw a stone high up in the air, but when it hit the water it made a decidedly stone-like sound.

*You see, he gestured.

*Read to me from the newspaper.

She nudged his arm.

*Don't want to.

*Come on. Over here. It's very nice, look.

—All right, all right.

He sat down by the tree. This was a game they had. He unfolded the newspaper. Molly sat with her back against him.

—On the fourteenth of July, a man was discovered walking about in a daze near the courthouse. He claims to have been asleep *inside a hill* for the last fifteen years.

*Twenty is better.

—All right, twenty years, the last twenty years. He was greatly confused by the gray banners everywhere, and by the change in administration. He has been taken by the police for questioning. It is believed he is pretending, and that he didn't actually sleep inside a hill.

*That's no good, said Molly. Don't have it be pretending.

—All right, let's try it again.

He removed his hat and set it on the ground next to him, then cleared his throat.

—On the fifteenth of July, a man was found in a confused state near the courthouse building. He claims to have been asleep *inside a hill* for the last twenty years. Upon further investigation into the matter, authorities have discovered the hill in question, and, within it, a sort of foxhole. The man refused to comply with any questioning, and escaped through the faucet of a sink. Beware!

Molly smoothed her dress, but did not smile. It wasn't her habit to smile at things that were funny.

*That's the news, then.

And all of a sudden it was becoming dark. The lights bloomed automatically all along the streets, and at the edges of the lake. A bell rang, and it was a shift change. Workers could be seen exiting houses, and beginning on their way to the factories at the outskirts of the town.

*I wish you could play for me a piece where you can hear the curtains blowing. Where you scrape the strings and the curtains move.

—Don't talk like that.

Molly pushed against him.

They threaded a path in a homeward direction, he murmuring, she gesturing, he peering at her hands in the dim evening.

^

When they reached the street there was a crowd formed around a man who seemed to be asleep on the ground. He was in a mime's regalia, with painted face and thin gloves. Suddenly he sprang up and froze at attention.

In the street, another mime, marching as a soldier, passed by. Marching, marching, marching, and on the sixteenth step, he went on all fours and loped as a pack of wolves does, grimacing and showing row after row of teeth. He turned upon the crowd and made for them! Shouting and confusion. The single mime began to conduct an orchestra, and of a sudden, the soldier-mime was playing instruments of every description, alternating in rows on invisible seats with invisible instruments. The conductor mime sat in the invisible audience, dabbing a handkerchief at tear after tear.

A shout then,

—They are coming!

—Watch out! Run!

The orchestra threw its instruments in the air and careened madly off into the park. Yes, two men in shabby clothing ran off into the trees.

*Will they get away?

Molly's hand was very tight clutching at William's coat.

*Will they get away?

—They have gotten away. That's how they did it in the first place. That's why, even if they get caught, they can't be caught. It wouldn't mean anything, other than to show that they are what they say they are.

Molly frowned.

—They are students, said William. It is their resistance and has at its heart their youth. Catching them only makes others join them. So, in a sense, they want to be caught. Or be at the edge of being caught, always.

*They don't want to get away?

—No, not really.

*But if they were caught, wouldn't they be . . .

—Yes, it is a choice they are making, to be alive and unrepentant.

*Unrepentant?

—They don't want to have to ask permission for anything, least of all for being alive.

*But could they win? What would that be, if they won?

Molly looked at William inquisitively.

—There are always different types of resistance. These are of one type. Their resistance is both to the government and to the world in general, to existence, to just being, also. There are others who want to . . .

He leaned in close and whispered in Molly's ear.

—overthrow the government directly and put something else in its place. That's why so many people have been dying.

*What would they change?

—For one thing, you wouldn't have to go to that particular school anymore.

Molly clapped her hands together excitedly.

*When do you think it will happen?

—Oh, I don't know. Something terrible would have to happen first.

Molly thought about that a little and then she thought about that some more, and then they were back at the apartment and William was moving about, switching on the lamps.

＾

—I am going to meet some people. It's important, and so I have to do it. You will eat supper with Mrs. Gibbons. I'm going to speak with her now about it.

Molly said nothing, but stared up at him.

—You really must go along with it.

Molly continued simply staring at him.

—I mean to say, it's the best thing. We can't have you here all alone.

Molly covered her face and, turning her back to him, sat on the floor.

—See here.

He picked her up and began to say how there was nothing to worry about, something sweet and meaningless like that. But he did not say it.

Instead,

—My dear, we must remember how the elephants behave.

Molly collected herself and came along immediately, but balked suddenly and threw herself on the floor.

—What is it?

*Just remembered something.

She was pointing her hand at William, while still lying prone on the floor.

—What did you remember?

*Elephants are playful. They do not *behave*. They must not.

—So what would a compromise be?

*You know.

—There isn't time.

*Just a short one. Short!

A SHORT GAME of THIS & THAT

which is a game of clues hidden among things in the house, woven in messages and riddles.

It was a family inheritance and Molly adored it above all things.

—You go sit by the window and ONLY look out.

Molly grumbled silently.

—Go on.

*Going.

William found a pad of paper, a scissors, string, and a pencil. He sat on the edge of the table and surveyed the room.

How to begin?

There was a photograph of a little bird falling out of a nest. That's a good place to start, eh?

William wrote then the first instruction:

———————————

A person leaves the house by an unfamiliar route. If something had been left behind, where would you look? Behind?

———————————

He continued his work, and occasionally the sound of the clock came and hurried him in his labors.

FINALLY, done! A breeze was entering the room through the window and rushing about inside, giving small notice here and there. William would have smiled then, had he been the sort to smile. One envies such types—who do not smile. The rest of us go around like fools, and these few maintain such dignity! Let us never smile again.

—Molly.

(She spun around and hopped down from the windowsill.)

—Here.

A piece of paper, neatly drafted.

THE SIXTH THIS & THAT

by W. for M. late in the day.

beginning on the table, you should know

Molly ran to the table and snatched up the paper.

It read:

A person leaves the house by an unfamiliar route. If something had been left behind, where would you look? Behind?

She began to walk up and down the room, brow bent, hand tapping against the skirt of her dress. All the while her other hand chattered to itself.

*Aha!

At the photograph of the bird's nest,

she stopped. Reaching up, she lifted the frame. A note on a string dropped down. Out she took it.

It said:

If dogs were wild once, then I too am wild. If a rifle consists of circles within circles, then I too circle. I am an old measure, made by a king, and when people speak of me, they have forgotten who I am.

Molly frowned. She looked around suspiciously.

*Don't know about this.

William took an orange from a basket by the stove, peeled it, and ate a section.

Molly continued in her suspicion. She did not walk this time, but stood moving her head ever so slightly from right to left.

*Another clue?

—How many clues do you need?

*Seems like one more, doesn't it?

William ate another piece of orange.

Molly sat down and immediately jumped up again. From the back of her shoe, she tore the next note and string.

*You, you stinker.

This note said:

Loons out under indelicate skies abate.

Molly walked slowly to the windowsill and sat. She held the note up to the light. She turned it upside down. She put the corner in her mouth. She pulled it taut. She tossed it in the air and watched it fall. She picked it up again.

—It's a good one, don't you think?

*Too hard.

William shook his head. He thought then of his violin teacher, long dead.

There was a long oaken drive dancing between the road and the house and the shadows were mad for the trees and the sun and raged there as William ran to the house in those emptied years, summers, mornings, days. It was a hard discipline she had, and she would hurt him awfully, and his parents approved of it all, but she made him feel he was her main work, and raised him above all other things, explaining music to him not in terms of other things, but in their absences, in the places where things meet. A sonata is not the passing of geese, it is not a stream's noise, not the sound of a nightingale. A violin does not speak, does not chatter. The catastrophe of a symphony's wild end is not a storm breaking upon land. It is not the shuddering and sundering of a house. But it is in part, she would say, the understanding of these things. You must be brutal, terrible, but with great sympathy, sympathy for all things, and yet no mercy. Was that why the government wanted no music? Because music was the only thing with any religion to it?

In the night (for it was night now) a low keening sound came. William closed his eyes. It was the sound of the bridge vibrating in the distance. The wind must strike it just so, and then . . .

*Aha! I know!

And William was back in the room again.

Molly ran across, clattering and stamping, to where . . .

a PICTURE of LOUISA was on a HOOK.

And from the picture frame, she pulled a string. And on the string, a note.

In the picture, Louisa was standing in the foreground, holding a kite. William was sitting in a tree farther in. A long field stretched into the distance.

Molly was holding the note but looking at the picture.

*You said it would never fly?

—Never. We called it the Sledge, because it would always drag along the ground. No one could get it to work. Although to be fair, I never managed to get any kite to work.

*What about Mom?

—I never saw her operate a kite. She held one once. Someone else had gotten it into the air, though. I don't think that counts.

*Doesn't.

Molly opened this note.

———————

Here we incarcerate the song and the one who makes it.

———————

Molly spelled it out.

*Incarcerate?

—Jail.

She ran to the birdcage (which was empty) and pulled out the next clue.

—This is the last one, said William.

Molly waved him off, and opened the note.

IT READ:

———————————————

Once the province of lords, and at once, a favorite of beasts, I delight as sugar does, but sate as water. Skinned, just as you, I hang and await my turn, and drop to the merciless ground.

———————————————

*Sate?

—Rid of hunger or thirst.

*Province?

—Look it up.

Molly went to the dictionary, opened it, and found the word.

*Doesn't make it much clearer, does it?

—No complaints now. I have to go. Solve it!

Molly's eyes roamed the house and alighted upon the basket of fruit. She ran to it.

*The orange!

She picked up the first orange, but there was no note there. Nor on the second.

Then she spied the orange that William had been eating. He had peeled it perfectly and the round skin sat on the table. She snatched it up and it fell open in connected rings, revealing a white bead made of bone.

Molly untied the necklace she was wearing and strung the bead onto it. There were five already there. This was the sixth.

—Time, then, he said, and ran his hand through her hair.

William went to the door of their apartment and opened it in a slow, sweeping fashion, eyes down. Molly joined him there. He went through, and to the door opposite, and knocked three times.

Noise came from inside. Someone was coming to the door.

—Hello?

The door opened. It was a woman in her seventies.

—Would you mind, asked William, watching Molly for a few hours? I have to go out, and I can't take her with me.

—I will do this, said Mrs. Gibbons. You are a good father and I will do this for you and your daughter because she is very wonderful, a very wonderful young woman and I am always glad to have her here, although she has not come before. There is always a place here in the house for a wonderful young woman who goes around with the name of Molly. But you must be careful, Mr. Drysdale, if you are going out at night, because I will tell you that Mr. Gibbons, who has just come home now this very moment, he told me that he saw a man dead not four streets over, and right in a crowd. So, you have a care. The ones who enforce the curfew, they are all at once watching everyplace both here and there. This man I say was dead, and that is one way that is always the same, dead.

William looked over his shoulder. Molly's face was a bit drawn.

—Dead? he asked.

—Yes, hit with a brick. And the one who did it couldn't be found.

Molly stamped her foot. William looked over.

*Be careful!

She went past him and into Mrs. Gibbons's apartment.

—Here is a key, said William, so you can put her to bed.

Mrs. Gibbons nodded and shut the door.

He could hear her:

—A good girl like you should not make your father worry. You do not do anything to make him worry, do you? No, I thought not. I thought not. Well, would you like something to eat? Come with me.

THE CURFEW

had been in place both when the police could be seen and now when they were unseen. One could not be about in the nighttime past a certain hour. What hour that was many could not say. They simply stayed put in their houses and waited for the morning. There were others who went about secretly, skulking. Were some caught? Yes, and never seen again. The consensus was this: on a clear night, the point at which the moon becomes clear against the night sky—from this point on you were to be indoors. On a cloudy night, there was perhaps less latitude.

The government's official word on the matter was nonexistent. There was no curfew. There was simply the declaration, *GOOD CITIZENS PASS THEIR NIGHTS ABED.*

^

In the street, the lamplight made avenues beyond the door and paths within the walks beneath the trees.

William walked there and he thought of Louisa, and of the plans they had made. What does dying do to plans one makes with one's beloved? It is the advent of lost causes, of pointless journeys, empty rooms, quiet hours. He said this to himself, and he felt it was not right. It was true, but not right. We were to have a house ringed about by trees in the country, and we were to live there with no one nearby, and raise a daughter.

He had never seen Louisa dead. She had been removed, taken from the street. Her father had been a politician. He had always guessed that was the reason.

All his inquiries to find her had met with no success. Louisa Drysdale? We have no record of a Louisa Drysdale.

The day she disappeared it seemed impossible. He walked up and down in the house. He sat in the stairwell. He went down to the street and up again. He turned on the stove and turned it off. Finally, it happened that he was asleep, and then it was the morning and he woke and at first thought it was a dream, but it was not, and then he was looking for her again, but there was nowhere to look, and all the while he was terrified of trying too hard, of pushing too hard, and of being taken away himself and leaving Molly with no one. So, there had been days of waiting, expecting that she would return at any moment. But Louisa had not returned.

^

There was a redness on the right.

He came closer.

A building was on fire. Men were running out of it. It was a police station, it must be. The police no longer wore uniforms, but one could tell who they were, and whenever they stayed for a while in a single building, it was assumed that that building was a police station, and then someone set fire to it.

One could assume, therefore, that if a building was on fire then it might well be a police station.

∧

One thinks of the age when people died in winter, often, for no reason—or when children simply passed away without explanation or grief.

But is it true? Were they so hard who placed those small bodies in the earth? It is disputed—and though one may say, all is the same and relative, yet still clearly, there are some who are followed in the street by vengeful anger, a clothing they may never remove.

I said—life begins for some when it ends for others and in another century I might have died an infant. What sort of riddle is it to suppose the grief my death would have entailed? Is it not on the ground over that very grave that my life proceeds?

∧

—We tire differently if we love or love not. I was never tired when playing violin. I became exhausted. I fainted occasionally from practicing without eating and drinking. But I was never tired. Now I am almost always tired.

But he wasn't tired then, was he? No, not at all. He was a bit nervous. He was talking to himself. He passed a few streets, and found the right one.

There were lights on in the windows of the houses. He was in a neighborhood he hadn't been to before. It was all brick, lane houses and the like. No one was in the street.

He looked at his watch. He was a bit late. But there was the house.

Up the stairs and about to knock.

—HEY! YOU!

A head was sticking out of a window in the house opposite. It was Gerard.

^

—This is the house, called Gerard.

William crossed the street and went up to the door.

—I thought you said . . .

—I always give the wrong address, in case I'm over-heard. Then I watch for people to come. Knock. Some-one'll let you in. I'm coming down.

^

He stood there before the house and it was as though someone shouted to him to not go in—as though he was gripped by hands and pulled away—as though,

but rather no one was there. The street was quiet. Was he shaking? There were lights in the windows of this and every other house, of many houses he had seen. Light that comes in bursts and falls. Persisting relentlessly, in showers of sparks. Could it be that light was a false hope and had ever been? That would be the death of anyone— to recognize false hopes with a certainty. One mustn't know that. If it is offered, refuse!

PART 2

IN THE APARTMENT

—I think that what is most needed for you, young lady, is that a puppet show should be made, and by you, and that my husband he will do a great job of helping you with it, because, do you know, he was making puppets in his old work, although now he does not.

Molly nodded gravely.

—Come on, he's in here.

The apartment was full of objects: cookie cutters, quilts, photographs of long ago, a sewing machine, a pressing machine, a long pole with metal bands at either end.

Mrs. Gibbons took the pole and put one end in a slot on the ground. The other end she slid into a port on the door.

—You'd need an army to bust down that, said Mrs. Gibbons. Come now.

Molly followed her into the next room, where Mr. Gibbons was sitting in an armchair.

—There's a job for you, Mr. Gibbons, to help this Molly here to make a puppet show. Now I want you to do it properly as you used to and not spare a thing. It's a serious matter, you know, and it's Molly's first visit here.

—Well, don't I know my own business, Mrs. Gibbons. Come here, young lady. We'll sit and talk a moment about what sort of puppet show you want to make.

Molly looked back and forth at Mrs. and Mr. Gibbons. She tried to sign *I don't speak.

—The poor thing, said Mrs. Gibbons. And me not knowing sign language, either.

—Well, that's the least of our worries. Here's a sheet of paper.

Mr. Gibbons produced a pencil and a piece of paper.

—This'll do just fine, he said. You can sit here, Molly, and let's talk about this puppet show.

*I am very eager to do the puppet show and also think it's kind of you to have me here. I and my father are very grateful.

—Oh, it's nothing at all. You needn't worry yourself.

Mrs. Gibbons went out of the room and called back in:

—I'll be coming with something hot to drink in a while, and ask the girl has she had supper.

—Have you had supper, Molly?

*Haven't.

—Hasn't, but would like to, I think, Mrs. Gibbons.

—That'll do, that'll do.

—A puppet show, said Mr. Gibbons, is a very delicate thing.

He sat on the ottoman across from Molly, and spoke with his hands. His face was reddish colored, and he wore a bathrobe over thick flannel pajamas. His eyes were very blue.

—I should know, he continued. Wasn't I the impresario of the famous Antediluvian Puppet Brigade? So, if you follow me, we'll go into the next room, and perhaps you'll get an idea or two. Be sure to take your paper with. And don't worry about using it up. Speak your mind. We've plenty of paper.

*I think a puppet show about music.

—Music, eh.

Mr. Gibbons's face assumed a serious expression.

—That's a large matter, especially now. I'm beginning to see the sort of girl you are.

They went together into the next room.

THE NEXT ROOM

housed at one end a beautiful puppet theater. The windows of the room were covered over with thick drapes that were nailed in at many points. There were about fifteen chairs to compose an audience. The theater was made of wood, and was raised off the ground. There were steps leading up to it from the side. On one wall, to the left of the theater, a long curtain hung. Mr. Gibbons threw it aside.

Many shelves were beneath it. The first shelf held tools of every description. The second held paint, and feathers, bits of fur and wood in shapes and sizes. Also, string in balls and tangles. The third and fourth and fifth and sixth held puppets, oh such puppets as Molly had never seen. There were kings and princes, sheep and lions, dogs and sheep princesses, wolves and mules, wolf kings and fox maids, tailors and churls and musketmen. There were crones and çat crones, wizards and haughty courtiers. But there were no children.

*No children? wrote Molly.

—There are never child-puppets in puppet shows, said Mr. Gibbons. Children must imagine themselves to be all the puppets, and can't afford to just feel they are the child-puppets. Besides, when disastrous things happen to the other puppets, it is all right, but it is very difficult for children to see disastrous things befall children.

*And animals.

—That's true, but at least then it stays in the imagination and doesn't stick in the heart as fear.

Mr. Gibbons had the talent that many puppeteers have of speaking to children as though he believed they were intelligent and could understand a thing or two.

—So, he said. What do you think?

Molly put down the piece of paper and signed for three minutes straight, all the while staring very seriously right at Mr. Gibbons. At the end, she did a little hop, and took up the pencil and paper again.

—I feel I know just what you mean, he said. Well, let's get started. Here's how it will go.

HERE'S HOW IT WILL GO

1. You will decide whether your world has animals in it, or people, or both, and whether the animals behave as people or as animals, or as both.

2. You will decide whether there is magic or not, and if there is magic, if anyone knows that there is or not, and if anyone knows about it, whether they tell anyone or not.

3. You will decide how many of the puppets will die, and how, so that we can have it happen at the right spots in the show.

4. You will decide if you want the puppet show to be funny or not. The puppet show will always be sad, but it can also be funny in parts.

5. You will decide if the theme should be: marriage, sickness, enchantment, inheritance, or revenge.

6. You will come up with the name of the villain. All the other names come out of the villain's name. The villain's nature, even that comes out of the villain's name. The only thing that doesn't come out of the villain's name is the expression on the face of the puppet which will be

our hero or heroine. That we will paint last, when we know everything. It is likely to be a thin smile. That's my specialty, but we shall see.

7. The puppet show will be in three acts. We will talk about the puppet show forwards, and when we are done talking, we will write the puppet show backwards. Believe me, it is a good method.

8. We will think about extra tactics, like stalling when the puppet show is about to begin, so we can paint the features of audience members onto minor puppet characters as a nice surprise.

^

Mrs. Gibbons came into the room carrying a tray with a pot of tea and a pile of hot biscuits with butter and honey.

Mr. Gibbons gave his wife an annoyed look.

—We have a great deal to do here, and can't be bothered with this.

But Molly was already eating the biscuits. Mrs. Gibbons poured the tea into cups and left the room, shutting the door quietly.

Mr. Gibbons set out a variety of puppets for Molly to inspect, all the while humming to himself in a happy way. It was his belief that puppetry was as expressive as ordinary theater, and in fact perhaps more expressive. If one person can control every aspect of the performance, then nothing need be lost. Nothing! He looked up suddenly.

Molly was peering at him across an empty basket where the biscuits had been. An empty teacup was there, an empty pot of honey, and a little plate half full of butter.

She took a napkin from the chair next to her and wiped her hands very deliberately.

*Shall we start?

Mr. Gibbons nodded.

THE DOOR OPENED BEFORE WILLIAM AND WHO DO YOU SUPPOSE WAS THERE?

A young woman, in a nightgown. The straps were falling down, but it did not seem to concern her. And from farther in, a voice came.

—Who is it?

—It's a man, maybe thirty, thirty-five? Thin. In an old coat, hasn't shaved. Widow's peak.

—That's Drysdale.

—Is that him, really?

—Yeah, tell him to come in.

—Tell him yourself.

The young woman turned and walked away from the door. Gerard came down from the floor above. He appeared relieved. One could tell this because he removed a handkerchief from his right pocket, folded it, and returned it again.

—William, he said. You came.

—Did you think I wouldn't?

—Well, you know. At first we thought you and Molly were taken along with Louisa, but then someone said they saw you at the park in the lake district. That's where you live?

—That's where we live.

—Well, come in. Come in.

In the next room, perhaps twenty people were sitting around, drinking what looked like wine out of wine-glasses. They were the sort of people William & Louisa used to be in the habit of knowing, a crowd of elegant furniture, like the legs of a herd of gazelle taken together, and equally useless, when all things are considered.

—Is that wine? asked William.

—We have our small pleasures, and we have gotten away with it so far. A glass?

—I haven't had wine in so long. I, well, yes, thank you.

William accepted the glass. The man closest to him turned and stuck out his hand.

—James Goldman. You're William Drysdale, I heard Gerard say so a moment ago.

—That's right.

—A pity about the music. I was a violinist, too, actually, amateur, nothing like you, but I, well, I was a musician, too, and I suppose it's the same isn't it, for us both, not playing?

—I try not to think of it.

William's expression was pained.

—Of course, the man continued, it's not the same. I don't mean it that way, I guess, I, I just mean, it's hard to not play, damned hard.

—It is that, said William. It is that.

THE WAILING OF A SIREN, THEN

between the houses and along the streets. It brought a harsh electricity into William's stiffness. Was no one else worried?

He leaned towards the man next to him.

—Do you often go out past the curfew?

The man laughed.

—Of course not. I actually have never done it.

Another man, very young, was refilling people's glasses with a newly uncorked bottle of wine. He had a very thin moustache and wispy hair.

—We stay the night, always, always. There are positively rooms full of beds, wouldn't you know.

He went off through the room, extending his bottle and giggling.

—Out after curfew indeed. You'd be a madman!

—That's Salien, he's a tremendous talent in vaudeville. In secret, of course. But really . . .

The man touched William's sleeve.

— . . . I hope you're not intending to try to make it home. They've been doubling and redoubling. Far too dangerous. Go home in the morning. You're not a fool.

The woman next to James Goldman spoke up.

—Did you see the fire on the way?

There was a peculiar mood in the room—an enforced jollity. Everything must be tinged with a disdainful humor and accompanied by slight laughter. William disliked the whole thing.

—A fire? said a bald man standing by the window. Did you set it?

—Me, don't be ridiculous, Sean.

—Well, you're introducing the subject. There must be a reason for it.

—They're always fighting, James explained.

—I saw the fire, said William. I think the building burned to the ground.

—A victory, said the woman in a low voice.

—Shush, Clara. Don't talk like that, not even here.

Gerard came in.

—Come with me. I have something I want to show you.

James was whispering something to Clara. No one seemed to be paying any attention. William got up.

—All right, then.

At the back of the house, there was a door to an addition. This addition was only the length of a room and unheated. Gerard handed William a coat from a pile. He himself put on a coat. They sat on stools.

—Is everyone here involved? asked William.

—Involved?

Gerard laughed.

—The point is: information like that doesn't exist. Who is, who isn't involved: it doesn't matter. We simply spread the *method,* and people act on their own. They don't need to tell anyone.

—The method?

—The method. It's very simple. Everyone will soon have learned of it, through channels exactly like this. Just one person telling someone else, someone trusted.

—Is it that bad?

—If you're caught with it in writing, less than a page of text, you're shot. Interrogated, shot. Most people who get interrogated say the same thing, and it's true.

—What's that?

—They found a piece of paper. They don't know anything about it. But in this town, there hasn't been too much printing yet. That's the dangerous part, the printing. But it spreads by word, also.

—What is it?

William had been struggling with himself. He wanted to leave, to go home and forget about the whole thing. He could feel it, like a door opening out of sight. This was something he didn't want to know, or be a part of. But he was curious, yes he was, and he was lonely, too, and here he was sitting with Gerard, a man he had known many years, and they were talking. Also, he was wearing a coat that wasn't his, a leather coat such as he would never ordinarily wear. There were things in the pockets, but he did not look to see what they were.

—Do you remember the time we went boating, you and Louisa, Ana and I?

William nodded.

—Do you remember when that man asked to take a picture of us, and Louisa didn't want him to? The man on the pier?

—I do.

—And then he took the picture anyway, and Louisa got angry, but we were already out in the current, and we didn't want to turn back. I sometimes think . . .

Gerard had taken the bottle with him. He took a swig from it.

—I sometimes think if we had gone back, then, everything would have changed, and she wouldn't have been shot.

William's mouth was dry. The idea of Louisa was all close spaces, distances, thick smells. It was inaccessible like the inside of a stone.

—What is the method? he asked.

—The method for disgovernance. Other revolutionary movements fail when they are found out. This one just begins when it is found out. It is impossible to stop because there are no ringleaders. It is simple enough to describe in a phrase or two the whole extent of it. Any member of the government, any member of the police, of the secret police, all are targets. You live your life, and do nothing out of the ordinary. But if, at some moment, you find yourself in a position to harm one of the targets, you do. Then you continue on as if nothing has happened. You never go out of your way to make such an opportunity come to pass. Not even one step out of your way. And yet, without exception, the targets must each day place themselves in danger before the citizenry, and cause such opportunities to exist. One doesn't prepare oneself, except mentally. One never speaks of it, except to spread the idea, and that is better done by sheets of paper left here and there.

Gerard was silent for a minute. He drummed his hand on the table. He took another sip of wine.

—The perfect crime consists of randomness: you happen to be passing a table on which a diamond necklace is lying; everyone has momentarily turned away; you snatch the necklace and continue; you are now the possessor of a diamond necklace. Having randomly arrived there, you had every reason to be in that place at that time, as part of your routine. You only ceased, in the moment of the crime, to be a thing apart from the background, and immediately thereafter, you returned to it. The only thing the New State can do is to clamp down tighter, and that only earns them more hate, activates more of the population. The method is reaching us here only now, but it has been around for two years. And a year ago, do you remember what happened?

—They disbanded the police. Now, only secret police.

—Exactly, and they never said why. But a man I spoke to . . .

The door opened and a woman stuck her head through.

—Gerard, can you come? I'm trying to convince Leonard that there's a growing sentiment abroad, but I can't remember all the figures.

—In a minute.

—All right.

She shut the door.

—This man said that they moved the police force entirely into plainclothes because in another sector, the police were getting mowed down. A policeman couldn't walk down a street without being hit by a slate tile. First they tried making the police paramilitary, with jeeps, etc. But ultimately, to do the job, they have to get out of the jeeps, and then the same opportunities present themselves. It's a matter of patience, and decisiveness. The point is, we're winning. It's only a matter of time.

—But how do you know who the police are?

William thought of his conversations with Oscar. It was virtually impossible to tell.

—You err on the side of false positives. Everyone shifts their behavior to simple routines, and the secret police are forced to become visible, simply to do their work. Then they become available as targets.

The ringing of a bell could be heard in the distance. The room had become very quiet. Gerard was looking at William and William, he was looking at Gerard. Louisa was not there, for she was dead, but in that way she was in fact there.

—Shall I say it? said Gerard.

William nodded.

—Someone I know, who was, well, he was working for the government then, before he came over. He saw what happened to her. I can't relate it. I don't want to. But I have everything about the file here.

He produced a folder from behind one of the boxes and handed it to William. It was tied around with string and was quite thick.

—I imagine you'll want to look at that at home, or somewhere without company.

The door opened again.

—Gerard, will you come?

—All right, here I am. Hold on a moment.

He stood up.

—Well, that's it, William. I wanted to show you something else, too, but I guess it can wait.

—What is it?

The girl pulled on Gerard's arm.

—Hold on, he said.

He knelt down and opened a cabinet that was on floor level. Out of it, he removed a flat black leather case. He set it down.

William could feel his pulse in his hands.

Gerard unfastened two buckles and opened the case.

It was a violin.

—Where did you get it?

—Can't say.

William looked at the girl.

—Don't worry about me, she said. I'm the one who got it.

—It's for you, William, said Gerard. You should probably go home now. Having you here, it's out of the routine, and a danger for both of us. You have a safe route home? You planned it, no?

—I . . .

William looked away.

—Perhaps it's best you stay, then. If you don't have transportation, or a clear route. I thought you had, well, don't worry about it. Just stay. If you don't want to be among people, you can read upstairs in the bedroom, and leave first thing.

—I have to be home. My daughter, you see.

—I see.

∧

William paused a moment on the stair.

In one hand he had the violin case, in the other the scrip
of files.

Laughter came from within. William shook his head.
The lights along the streets blinked on then off.

^

Gerard shut the door and watched the figure go away along the street, the black case apparent under his arm.

—Do you think he'll . . . ?

—He won't play it, not ever. But at least he will have it.

—And for the rest?

—If he acts, if he doesn't, it's meaningless. The whole thing goes forward. No one is important. No one at all.

—A war with no participants. Only casualties. The forest opens and consumes the troops.

She laughed.

—And consumes the troops, agreed Gerard.

She came to the door and stood beside him looking out the window.

There was nothing to see.

—I have a terrible feeling, he said. Like the rope isn't tied to anything.

—Come now, he'll make it home. Come.

She kissed him and led him back to the others.

^

—And here, said Mr. Gibbons, is the brush I always use for eyes.

He handed Molly an extremely thin brush.

—It is not a-single-horse's-hair, but it is close to that.

Molly wrote on the paper:

*Three horse hairs?

—Perhaps.

The brush had a furious red handle. Such a handle, it seemed that it would grant life to whatever it made. Molly gave it back to Mr. Gibbons reluctantly.

*But why a different brush for eyes? Is there one for mouths, for ears, for cheeks? Molly wrote.

Mr. Gibbons read the paper.

—You're a shrewd one, he said. That's for certain. Here's why: if I have to switch brushes for each feature, it grants me the space of thought. I can't just dash 'em off. Also, the brush can be acquainted with its specialty, if you believe such things.

He coughed.

—Not that believing such things has anything to do with whether they are true. You see that, don't you?

Molly nodded.

—The effect of irrational beliefs on your art is invaluable. You must shepherd and protect them. I'm sure your father would say the same.

*He believes many things.

—I'm sure he does.

Mr. Gibbons held up a puppet with a veiled face. It was a male puppet in a jester suit, but its face was veiled.

—There are puppets, said Mr. Gibbons, who know more than what the other puppets know. Do you see what I mean? Not all the puppets are privy to the same information. This puppet for instance, this puppet, I save him for special circumstances. He is aware that the puppet show is going on, and of his place in it. That doesn't mean that he knows about the puppeteer, not exactly. His information, of course, is not always correct. However, he does know much more than any of the other puppets. Sometimes, why sometimes he can even see the audience.

Molly wrote something on her piece of paper and then crossed it out.

—That's right, said Mr. Gibbons. It's better to have something like that in your head awhile before asking questions about it. I quite agree.

—Once, he continued, in a play about a horse, this puppet, this very puppet, explained to the cast that they were all being used, manipulated, made fools of. On the spot, right there, the puppets refused to go on. It was a disaster. I had to refund all the show's proceeds. The audience left in a huff.

Molly smiled and took a long breath. She scribbled down a question.

*He can say things to them in one play and they won't know it in the next. Everything starts over, no?

—Everything starts over. Except—maybe, just maybe, he has some sense of the history of all these puppet shows. That's why he sits here, on this fine throne, over-looking the whole room.

It was true that the veiled jester had a fine view of the room.

*What voice do you use for him?

—Oh, he has many voices. As many as the leaves on the tree he was carved from. He is a teller of stories, but a great liar as well.

*But isn't one *his* voice?

—Well, we will just have to see if he joins the play, won't we? Time passes. We must continue our good work. Come over here now. We must make some of those decisions I spoke of.

^

William went along the street as quickly as he could. To run would be foolish. It would attract attention. Besides, it was too far. He could never run all the way. But walking below a certain speed was foolish, too—it meant someone walking behind and faster might overtake you. So one had to walk fast enough to not be overtaken, but not fast enough to arouse suspicion. Also, if it seemed that one might overtake someone else, one had to choose a route to pass by the person without suspicion.

The papers in his hand burned at him. He wanted to tear open the papers right then, but knew that to get home was most important.

The noise of footsteps came from up ahead. William ducked into the entranceway of a building. He reached up and unscrewed the lightbulb. He was in darkness, and across the way the streetlight blinked on and off. The footsteps were nearer now. He was positive he could not be seen, but still his hands shook.

I must get home, he said to himself. I must get home to Molly.

There were three men and they were talking loudly. They were upon him and then past him. He watched them go. These men were not worried in the slightest. But who could they be, to not be worried?

William hurried on.

∧

A fancy rose in his head then, that he would be caught, but that he could escape. He would be running and they would corner him in some stone court. They would be grim faced, terrible, and he would draw out the violin and play and his pursuers would be forced to dance and dance until it was morning. The sun would rise and they would collapse on legs that would not support them and he would hurry away home. He could play that well. He felt he could. He could feel their legs failing them, could feel them dropping one by one, helpless.

^

—It will be a musical play, said Mr. Gibbons, reading from the sheet Molly had handed him, but there will be little or no music in it.

He looked up.

—That's sound, he said, and in keeping with our resources. I see you have a brain in your head. Has your father spoken about music to you? No, no, don't answer that. I'm sure anything you have to say will appear in the play, and that will be enough for me.

He continued,

—It will not be a musical play, as in, a musical. Music is the theme.

He nodded.

—The characters will be divided between animals and humans. It will be clear that nothing in particular is meant by one being an animal or not. Although, of course, a particular trait associated with an animal might have a bearing on the character portrayed. E.g., a cunning fox, or a silly goose.

—There are no goose puppets anyway, said Mrs. Gibbons, who sat silently in the corner, knitting something indefinable.

—There will be no magic, whatsoever. Magic is either a poverty-stricken necessity or a wealthy fantasy. We are in neither of those straits, and what cannot be explained will be left unknown.

A glad tension had begun to show around the edges of Mr. Gibbons as he saw that it would be a real puppet show. Now, each proof that Molly made of her seriousness was joined with the forgotten vitality of his long life's puppetry.

—Death of puppets: still to be spoken of. Show: not funny. Theme: sickness (grand scale). Villain: none.

Here Mr. Gibbons drew up like a struck horse.

—I say, young lady, I really do, I must say, a puppet show with no villain. Why, we shall have to talk this through. I don't know that it can be done, and even if it could, well, why would you want such a thing, and then there is the matter of what is the glue to hold it all together, and how I have already been thinking of how it might be, and, Molly. I'm not sure this will do.

Molly stared up at him with determination.

He continued,

—Three acts, yes. Forwards, backwards, as you like. No audience, I suppose.

He put down the sheet and looked at her.

—As for the audience, well, we'll see about that.

He winked at Mrs. Gibbons.

—But for the rest, yes, let's talk over here where Mrs. Gibbons can't hear us.

Molly and Mr. Gibbons went to the far side of the room. A moment later, Molly returned for her paper, and dashed back again. From the corner, much scribbling and fuming.

∧

William had passed along four more streets and had been forced to hide twice more. Windows with a meager light might be seen at every crossing. He kept thinking of something Louisa had told him, shortly after they'd met.

—Sometimes the gladness of a candle is all there is to a room, and it's saved for the person who sees it from far away. Those in the room know nothing about it, and are sometimes themselves gone from the room, even while sitting there. Cold rooms. One doesn't want to be there, except when they've been misunderstood, as when seen from outside. We mustn't be that way.

He had assured her they would not. Looking back, there had been no danger of it. It was a strange thing, William thought, to be young now—he *was* young—and for Louisa to have been dead already years. To still be young. And all the many years still left. Too many. But for Molly, he would . . .

He ducked behind a tree. Two men, this time with flashlights. These were dressed in a military fashion. Some sort of night guard, and the only one who sees them is taken away. If he was in the situation, as Gerard had said, this situation that you are brought to by chance, would he be brave enough to act? Many things had suddenly made sense. All the recent trouble—it was due to an idea. A clean, clear idea. He had searched for such ideas, once, he and Louisa.

They were gone now. He came out from behind the tree and hurried on. It was a cold night. Against the houses ahead, he could see that the fire was still burning—had it been a police station?

Now, the last of it: he had to cross a broad stretch of pavement to get to his quarter. He broke into a run. It seemed a great distance he had to cover. It stretched away from him as he ran. He ran faster and it was farther.

—Hey, you! You!

William ran. He wanted to drop the violin, but it was useless. They would find it even if he dropped it, and he mustn't drop it. Yet more precious were the documents, and those would consign him to death regardless. He could not let them go, no matter what it meant.

Cries went up behind him. There were three, no, four of them. They were gaining. The black ground sped past him. Lights whirred in the distance.

—There he is.

They were on either side. He ran into the park, and down a path. The dim, glowing bulbs of the park seemed to multiply shadows. He might do it. He might get away. Then, onto uneven ground, a moment, a moment, and then his feet were out from under him. The violin case was lost, it, too, was in the air, and then he hit the ground. The papers were gone. A second later and a body crashed into him, pinning him. Where had the papers gone? He struggled to get free.

—He's here. I've got him. Here.

Rough hands were on him, and a great deal of weight. William lay, lungs heaving, face cut from the fall. He could not even see the people who had caught him. This was the sort of war they were in.

—I must get home. My daughter. I, I fell asleep. I didn't realize what time it was. I was working late.

There was no response.

He said it again,

—I must get home. I have a child.

—No one is out now who doesn't mean to be.

It was an awful voice. It gave nothing beyond itself.

—I, I beg you.

William tried to turn off his stomach, but the man pressed down harder. He could hardly breathe.

—The others will be here soon.

The hands that bent his own arm down into his back must belong to that voice, but for all that he knew, it could have come from anywhere. There was a creaking high up in the branches of the trees, and it would continue through the long night. It meant nothing, just that the wind was blowing. The action of a thing is the same as the naming of it—is, in fact, the real name. The trees creak and they are saying, *trees creak through the long night*. The long night—what is it? Trees creaking. There wasn't anything that tied life's moments together, except life. And when it was gone?

^

They were finishing their painting of the figures. They had been hours at it, or mostly Mr. Gibbons, who was an expert, and could fix a figure at a moment's notice and with no effort whatsoever. Meanwhile, Molly wrote the dialogue, the scenes, and slipped them back and forth for Mr. Gibbons's approval. They were doing it backwards as he had said, backwards, except for the final scene. It was the compromise they had reached.

There was a mouse whose face had been given the features of Molly, a mouse dressed in a yellow slip.

There was a man and he had been cleverly painted. He really did look like William, and Molly said as much.

Two bird-puppets bore an uncanny resemblance to Mr. and Mrs. Gibbons.

A wolf with a crown had been Molly's final, and most difficult, choice. She had run back to her apartment to fetch a photograph from her father's desk. Now it was a she-wolf, in a long dress, and it looked like Molly's mother.

*I don't remember her very well.

—That's all right. You remember who she was, and your father has spoken of her.

*He told me all about her.

—I know he has.

And so the work continued.

—The motion of the puppets, Mr. Gibbons explained, is too complicated to teach now. You will have to be satisfied with my doing it. After all, you wrote it all down, everything, and I understand it well. I have the voices as they are, and for the Molly-marionette, we have the boards.

There were boards on which was written each portion of the dialogue of Molly's puppet. They would slide out at the appropriate time.

Molly had been so caught up in the preparations for the play that she was astonished to find, when she turned around, that many of the seats of the theater were now full. Mrs. Gibbons had placed life-size puppets of various kinds throughout.

—Every theater, said Mr. Gibbons, must have an audience, no matter how small.

The lights dimmed.

—Seats, everyone.

Molly sat in the front. The theater rose up before her and engaged her entire field of view. A fine curtain hung across it. Gilt edges ran the length through the poised air. The wood was painted in expectation of certain delight, and that very delight and longing ran all through her as though she believed that answers might be found. If her father would return soon, it might well be through the agency of puppets as well as anything. It might certainly. Might it not?

—Seats!

Mrs. Gibbons settled herself in the back row.

—A LADDER OF RAIN AND THE ROOF BEYOND, a play by Molly Drysdale (mostly) and Siegfried Gibbons (hardly).

Molly's hand was signing something beneath the chair, but it could not be observed.

It was now early in the morning and William still had not returned.

PART 3

A

LADDER

OF RAIN

AND

THE

ROOF

BEYOND

A horse rides in on a horse's back. It is dressed as a colonial soldier. The movements of the horse are exactly like those of a horse.

—Those who know me not, know this, said the horse: there are things that must be said, and this is how we say them: without regard to safety, and saving nothing for last. Else the fire cannot last the night.

The horse rides away.

A voice says:

Louisa is approaching a small window that has been cut into a wall. She looks back. She appears to be sneaking. Her life has been so far a happy one. Educated at the best schools, given the best things, taken to the best restaurants. Journeyed abroad. An owner of horses. Taken up in airplanes. Rail travel. Widely read. She felt as many well-brought-up people do that her life is a collection, that she is always collecting. She is also very brave and although rather weak, objectively, is physically tough by virtue of a fierce will. She had once cut herself in a shop while looking at hunting knives. Instead of saying anything, she just put her hand in her pocket. Halfway home someone made her take it out and found that it was covered in blood. Her pocket was soaked. Rather than hurt, she was just embarrassed.

Louisa approaches the window. It is really very small. She looks through the window. It is not the sort of window that divides indoors from outdoors, but rather that more secretive sort of window which privileges one room over another. Into a grand auditorium she peers. A figure is on the stage. Over her shoulder, we can just see through the window the vastness of the room beyond.

CURTAIN

A grand auditorium. William stands, not on one foot, not on two. His feet appear to be bearing his weight, but it isn't true. In fact, all his attention is on the violin in his hands, which he is about to play. He looks up at a small window cut into the back corner of the room. Someone in the back of the audience is whispering, and this is what they say:

This is an auditorium without seats. There is a stage and fine carpeting, a place for seats, but no seats. There is tiering, and avenues up to doors, footlights. There is a figure at the window. She shouldn't be here.

CURTAIN

Several scenes then in which Louisa and William become acquainted with each other. She is the daughter of a prominent politician. He is a musical prodigy from humble origins. He is gentle and dark and unrelenting. She is witty and playful. Her speech is littered with references to philosophical figures and instead of arguing a point she will sometimes choose to point out that so-and-so has already shown that concept to be fallacious. She is an expert horticulturist, a hobby of her mother's that she took on as a child. She, however, has never mentioned this to William. He is desperately in love with her. They meet in odd places. They eat supper on the floor of the room he lives in. He sneaks into her house at night. They are daring and hopeful. They expect that they will soon be married.

Molly's mouth is open slightly. Her posture is raised, expectant. The theater could not be so many things, and yet it is. The puppetry is beyond all expectation. Who could believe that the puppets are not alive, that their movements do not originate there in their wooden frames beneath their finely sewn garments, their fur, their feathers? One has always understood what a puppet looks like, what it can do. But this is not that. Is it possible, wonders Molly, for the finest things to be hidden? To be hidden and never shared?

There was a light rainfall and then it cleared. The threat of the storm was such that everyone decided to stay in all day. Only two people went out of their houses. William was one of them. Louisa was the other. They had decided to go out in the rain, but there was no rain to go out in.

A sort of one-room schoolhouse. Out of it comes William. He walks to the front of the stage and sits on a bench. He is looking down at Molly. He appears very much to be her father. Behind her, the puppets in the audience shift uneasily in their seats. Mrs. Gibbons coughs. The schoolhouse has gone and now there is the entrance to a ferryboat. Louisa disembarks. She says, to no one in particular,

—I was not on a boat. I wanted merely to avoid pursuit.

Her walk is extremely graceful and menacing. She has the aspect of a wolf.

Molly remembers this, although she remembers little else.

Louisa sits on the bench beside William. They look well together. Light clapping from the audience.

—My conductor believes I should practice the most difficult parts by the lions' cage of the zoological enclosure.

—Have you tried it?

—Each time I become drastically better.

—Do you pay attention to their faces?

—The lions' faces?

Louisa is carrying something. It is a package of some sort. William becomes aware of it. They speak regarding the package. He takes it in his hands and opens it. On the stage, the puppet actually manages to utilize his appendages in order to open a sealed package using a small knife. Inside the package is a hat. He puts it on.

—In the band of the hat, says Louisa, is written the place of our next meeting.

She kisses him. They go off in opposite directions.

And . . .

In the distance, a crowd is waiting, painted onto the scenery. It is composed of everyone they will ever meet. Not a single person in the crowd can see the others, and they stand quietly, weight drifting idly from one foot to the other.

CURTAIN

The floor of the theater is painted like the ceiling of the sky as seen from above. The veiled puppet appears onstage.

Molly sits up straight. She looks around. The puppets behind her are all intent on the stage. Mrs. Gibbons's eyes do not stray either. A little light is at the edge of the shuttered window. Molly looks at her feet. She looks up at the stage again. The veiled jester is watching her.

—Molly, he says. The play must continue.

He gestures for the curtain to fall and it does. It opens again and the jester is gone. In his place is a grove of trees.

William and Louisa enter. It is somehow clear that Louisa is pregnant. They have been married and living together in a fine and upstanding fashion while William's concert career blossoms. Meanwhile, Louisa meets various disreputable intellectuals for confusing theoretical conversations. Both are happy. They are carrying a trunk. William has a shovel. He digs a hole and they bury the trunk.

—Our child will one day learn of this and find this place and gain possession of many of the key treasures of our early life.

They throw the dirt over. Louisa's skirt becomes filthy. She makes a joke about it, but William does not laugh. He is peering into the underbrush to be sure no one has seen the burial. He feels they are being watched.

CURTAIN

Someone is singing very quietly. Louisa is sitting by a cradle. The house is very much like an owl, or like the house of an owl. Through the window a soft light obscures her features. A door can be heard opening deeper in the house. Footsteps. The door to this room opens.

ENTER WILLIAM

—My dear, it took so long. I couldn't get away. The others didn't have their part exactly right, and you know how Werz is. He wouldn't let them off the hook. So we all had to sit there.

He and Louisa look down into the cradle. The cradle is empty. Molly is traveling towards it, but has not yet arrived.

—Do you know, whispers William, that when I was a young man I would never stay the full length of anything? I would go to a show and leave partway through. I would slip out of dinner parties, evening parties, breakfasts. I'd slip out and just wander off down the street, extremely happy. It became a sort of joke among my friends, but they could do nothing to stop it. I'm sure I offended some people, but they were probably people I didn't like in the first place.

The person is still singing, and begins to sing louder. It is impossible to say what the person is singing. William and Louisa can no longer be heard, although they are plainly speaking. Molly struggles to hear what they are saying, but she cannot. This part of her childhood is lost for a second time. She is on the edge of her seat.

The puppet show proceeds rapidly through the exposition. Molly cannot yet walk; she must be carried. Later, perhaps she can walk a bit. She and William and Louisa are often to be seen in the parks and on the long avenues. As they walk, the trees bend towards them, the grass stands up on long legs, the air convenes and disperses, making light breezes and zephyrs.

A man in a blue hat, Lawrence, comes to visit one day. The set is dark. It is the middle of the night. There is a knocking. A light comes on. Louisa gets out of bed. She walks down the set through various hallways and stairs, trailing the thinnest of marionette wires. At the bottom, the door and on it a fine brass knob. She touches it with her hand and makes as if to turn it.

—Who's there?

—Louisa, it's me. It's beginning. You have to get out of here. I'm leaving myself. Tell William. The musicians will be among the first to go. I'm sure of it. And you, certainly you know they'll never let you off.

She opens the door. The sight of a man in a blue hat confronts her. It is, in fact, Lawrence.

William joins them at the door.

—Lawrence, what are you talking about?

—News from out of town. They've set the congress on fire. The whole thing's begun. The army is with them. The whole thing's done. It's useless.

Lawrence runs out into the street. In the distance, the sound of something hitting a tin can.

Mr. Gibbons's face comes around the side of the house, impossibly large. He addresses the audience:

—That should be gunfire. My apologies. Please recognize it as gunfire. Once more.

He disappears. Lawrence is again at the door. Louisa is composed, but extremely disturbed. William looks angry.

—News from out of town. They've set the congress on fire. The whole thing's begun. The army is with them. The whole thing's done. It's useless.

Lawrence runs out into the street. He is holding his blue hat in his left hand. In the distance, the sound of gunfire.

William wraps an arm around Louisa. They shut the door. There is a painting there, and it draws the eye. The two pause there to inspect it, as if the answers lie therein.

It is a painting of a battle. There are rows of men with bright uniforms. There are cannon. Places have been dug out to foil the cavalry. Bodies are strewn between the various positions. The sky is bright in the distance, but dark overhead. A vulture is crouching on a colonel in such a way that it seems perhaps the vulture is the colonel. Nonetheless, it appears that the colonel is doing a marvelous job. He has won the battle. Why? The eyes of his troops are fierce and the others are as pale as mirrors. One can easily imagine the vast and beautiful columns of reinforcements arriving out of the east. The sound as they pound the road, as they draw nearer and nearer.

But for us there is no help, thinks William. He cannot say it, not to his wife. If he should do so, even once, it would immediately be true.

A voice:

—The next day conducted itself as usual; nothing had changed. There was no report of anything. Another day passed and another. A month passed. And then one day, soldiers marching up and down the streets. People hanged from telephone wires. The edicts posted. Interrogations of every kind along with new assignments of work. The whole thing turned on its head. The body of Lawrence found in a ditch outside town. He had lain there a long time before he was found. Compulsory attendance at so-called Section Meetings. A census conducted house by house. William and Louisa accepted the situation as best they could. William's instrument was taken. The symphony was no more. It was turned into a courtroom. There was suddenly a need for many more courtrooms than had previously existed. A portion of the citizenry previously given short shrift now rode high and composed the various juries of various courts that tried every imaginable offense. In fact, there were so many offenses that one couldn't avoid committing crime. One had to simply limit one's time in the public eye, accept small penalties. All manner of symbols denoting various crimes were worn on one's person. This was the period of transition. Things grew worse. The food shortages began. They had conversations, saying things to each other. He will say one thing and she will reply, or she will speak and he will answer. They reach out often without reason, and speak often without import. This is the nature of their concern.

And then one day

LOUISA was

TAKEN AWAY

FOR GOOD.

William is crying and pacing up and down in the rooms of his house. He does this for days, but the scene lasts one hour, with his quiet sobbing. In the next room a small mouse puppet is crying also, in an entirely different register. Meanwhile, in the street outside, people come and go. A group of men looking straight ahead. A boy with a brown paper bag. A dog with a blanket hung over its back. A car here or there, a bicycle. William is sitting on the clean bedspread, holding one of Louisa's dresses. He is not pressing it to his chest, he is simply holding it. Mrs. Gibbons begins to cry softly, and the puppets begin to cry, one by one. The whole room is sobbing, except Molly, who sits bolt upright. Her hands are clenched. The next scene is about to begin.

CURTAIN

A BOARD WITH WORDS ON IT:

END OF ACTS ONE and TWO

and

INTERMISSION

A minute passes. Molly turns around in her chair. Mrs. Gibbons is missing.

—Pssst. Molly.

Molly sneaks a look over her shoulder. Mr. Gibbons, beside the theater, is motioning to her. She tiptoes over. The puppets look in a different direction.

—What do you think?

Molly pulls a scrap of paper out of her pocket.

*So far so good.

She pauses.

*Do you . . . You know, my father . . .

Looking over her shoulder as she is writing, he:

—I don't know. We'll just have to see.

*But . . .

—I wish I knew. I . . .

Into the room, then, Mrs. Gibbons with a mug of chocolate for each of them.

—TO YOUR SEATS, shouts the bailiff, he upon the highest turret of the theater.

Molly catches the edge of Mr. Gibbons's mouth moving, just by chance, as her eyes haven't left him. Ventriloquism, she thinks. And if he uses his ventriloquism to say my words through the mouth of another—what is that called?

She scratches her leg and hunches her shoulders.

—TO YOUR SEATS!

ACT THREE: to be conducted by LOTTERY of MEMORY.

The curtain sweeps open. The veiled jester is again upon his floor of clouds.

—I shall explain, he says. It will all soon be clear.

Each time he speaks with a different voice. Now he speaks with the voice of a scholarly nun calling a pupil to task.

—Molly. Molly! Come here.

Molly comes out from the side of the stage. Her tail is very long and gray. She walks on her hind legs and wears very delicately embroidered clothing. Her feet are clad in dancing slippers.

—Will you say a few words for the audience?

*There are certain days that shape a person's life because they change a person's understanding about what is possible in a day. This is why it is very important, for instance, as a child, to visit the house of a talented painter. I am speaking of a man or a woman who lives alone, knows no one, and paints while rivers and streams pass effortlessly in the vicinity unimpeded in a country of small bridges, lamps, and messages delivered by hand. My father brought me in secret to such a woman. She lived in the country and, being a hermit, was undetected by the revolution's machinery. Her house was a series of cottages linked by little paths through the woods. She would sit and watch the light as a hunter watches a deer path—for days before she would act. And then, all at once, the circumstances imprinted upon the paper as if stamped with inked steel. Her work was all shadows and faint colors. My father said she was his violin teacher. She did not play the violin, or any other instrument, and, in fact, could not speak. Here is the painting she gave to me.

Molly opens the secret chamber of a brooch and takes out a square of paper. It unfolds eight times. From the side of the theater, an enormous magnifying glass draws out and slips into place.

One by one the members of the audience rise from their seats and inspect the painting. Molly gazes a long time. The shading, the shadows, the fragile hues: all as she remembered. It is a painting of a collapsed building. Underneath a shattered floor, someone has built a fire. That person's back is to us, and he is reading a tiny leather book. The book is open on the palm of his hand.

Even the words of the book are visible, and these say:

Your trials will one day finish. You are young and will outlive your torturers.

CURTAIN

The audience returns to its seats.

THE CURTAIN SWEEPS OPEN

—It was a lovely day and it began well. There was a vendor selling nuts at the edge of the escarpment. They climbed past the ruined fortifications and walked on grassy ridges where small bushes claimed sovereignty. Ants ran like mice about their feet. They were ants! Ants dressed as mice. And in this, the machinery of the puppet show reveals its hand.

William and Molly come out onto the stage. She moves hesitantly. She is young yet, and somewhat fearful. William holds her hand firmly in his own, and is careful when shutting doors to be sure her tail is all the way through.

Up the slope of the fort they go, and there indeed is the nut vendor. They buy nuts and walk some distance to the shade of a single tree. There are ants, then, with little bits of fur glued to their carapace, that scurry about on the stage.

*Do you think, says Molly to her father, that this fortress repelled any grand attacks? Or was it always just landscape without human function?

—Look around for bones, says William. Then you'd know.

*Not if they were very neat about caring for their dead.

—There is no agency of neatness capable of finding all the casualties after a battle, declaims William.

Reaching behind the tree, Molly produces a long bone. A fateful impression comes over her. Even when this bone was the leg of a man, it nevertheless was awaiting its intended use. It was privy to this knowledge from the beginning.

William takes out a little knife. He holds the bone gently on his knee and sets to carving. He carves awhile and then rubs delicately with a small gray cloth and then carves awhile more. He is very fine in his motions, as if he has done this before. This is one of his talents—to appear accomplished when just beginning.

Molly runs about.

He presents the bone finally to Molly. On it is a long series of arcane directions.

—This is how to find a thing we hid, your mother and I. Keep it safe. These directions will not be accurate for another fifteen years. Then they will lead you straight where you need to go.

Molly tucks the bone under her arm. William hefts her up onto his shoulder and, taking the bag of nuts under one arm, walks homeward.

CURTAIN

A chair has been continually scraping. Molly turns around. It is a large pheasant puppet in a topcoat. He looks Molly right in the eye and sniffs.

She waves to Mrs. Gibbons. The pheasant is removed immediately.

Despite her quick action, Mrs. Gibbons appears somehow complicit.

AND

OH

HOW

TIME

HAS

PASSED!

A beautiful day, as anyone can see. The light is shining with brave intensity upon the springtime. Molly is older now, and walking ahead of William. She is signing out her multiplication tables and he is nodding or correcting as needed. They pass along the set, and as they do, the set itself changes. First they are in one street, then another. Time passes. The angle of the sun shifts. They arrive at the gates to the cemetery. William unlocks the gate with a long key that hangs like a sword from his belt. In they go. He intends to show her many of the epitaphs he has written. The paths in the cemetery are long and winding. The trees are ancient and well cared for. Moss abounds. Weeping willows are used judiciously to separate sections and give meaning to various points of prominence. Obelisks are strictly banned, or were at some point in the distant past. Those few that are evident predate the ban. They are so old that they can no longer be read. Their greatness shines no light on the ones they were meant to memorialize.

—Here, says William, is one of the very first I did.

A small stone, surrounded by tree stumps.

Elinor Gast

Drowned.

Molly stares at the stone for a long time.

—It wasn't true, actually, says William. She died of a heart attack. Her husband felt it would be exciting for the both of them, however, if the stone said *drowned.* It was his idea, entirely. That's what really established the tone of my epitaphry.

*And the next?

—Over here.

They cross a little bridge over a stream and come to a grove of sycamores. The entire Eldritch family in rows and circles.

*Let me see if I can find it, signs Molly.

She goes around from grave to grave. Finally, she shakes her hand up and down.

She and William inspect the stone together. It reads:

ELDRITCH

Mara   Colin

A short, hurtful dream.

---

*Who exactly did you speak to about this one?

—The husband's father, an extremely old man.

*He didn't care for his daughter-in-law?

William pats Molly affectionately on the shoulder.

—You could say that.

They hold hands and continue through the cemetery. The figure of the veiled jester can be seen watching them from behind a distant tree.

Now they are passing under a ridge of pines. There are small pink stones, roughly square, with little crosses blooming from their tops. Molly pauses and kneels by them. Her tail wraps around one. There is a sound from across the cemetery, the ringing of church bells. Her ears perk up.

—Soldiers, all, says William. Dead in the same blast of gunfire.

And indeed they had all died on the same day.

—But this isn't my work, says William. Long before my time.

Up the next hill they go. There at the top is a little stone house. In the house, a marble bench and a bare window. The window looks out across a stretch of the cemetery and the river. Part of the old city wall is visible where it once ran.

———————————

Ignazio Porro, who invented prism binoculars.

———————————

—That's right. I believe that's actually true.

There is a stone sculpture of a pair of binoculars on the floor near the window.

Molly tries to pick them up. They won't budge.

—Come on.

—Do you know, says William, when I was a young man I expected that I would never marry.

*Not ever?

—Not even your mother, said William. But your mother, you know, she was always asking me to go with her walking in rainstorms. It was her very favorite thing to do, to feel the rain and see the flashing of lightning. *They are hiding in their houses, see them,* she would say.

And we would go on running over the canal, and there was a song she would shout out.

William's voice trails away. He is speaking, but the sound has gone.

As they exit the little house, a face peers in from the other side. It is the jester. Molly and her father leave the stage. The jester climbs in the window.

—Molly, he says. Molly. They are all asleep. Look around.

Molly looks behind her. Sure enough, the puppets in the audience are all sleeping. Some have fallen off their chairs. The heads of others lounge oddly upon their chests. Mrs. Gibbons is dozing in the corner.

Molly signs:

*It means nothing. Continue.

The puppet stares at her without understanding.

She writes on a piece of paper:

*CONTINUE.

The puppet laughs.

CURTAIN

Molly is thinking about trees. Her tail curls and uncurls.

*What remains of a tree in a violin?!

—That's the permission, he says—but it is not in *every* violin.

*Nor perhaps, says Molly carelessly, in every tree.

To the south there is a passage of birds, thin but stretching on. Molly tears at the grass with her hands and the smell is thick and fresh. They are in the shade, these two, and never farther from the world.

—Yes, says William. It is farther than it seems.

They pass along a way through elms and with leaping on the roots of enormous maples—such and soon they are in another place.

Yes, Molly and her father are sitting in a dell, surrounded by pale brown stones.

—This is your mother's family, says William.

The stones are all in a different language.

*What do they mean?

—I don't know, says William. I never learned her parents' language. She didn't either.

*Strange for her to be here, surrounded by unknown sentiments.

—Well,

*I know, she isn't really here.

—Not really.

They walk to the last grave on the right. This is the finest one of all. It is as simple as a stone could be, almost rough, but with lovely texture. The letters in it are thin. Even fifty years will be enough to efface them.

Molly is coughing. She is coughing and coughing and making a peculiar sound. It must be the noise of her crying. Mrs. Gibbons wakes and comes up the aisle, kneels next to her, holding one of her hands.

William and his daughter leave the stage.

CURTAIN

Molly and William are asleep. The window to the street is open. There is a gunshot. They sleep on. Time passes. They wake. Molly dresses. The two go out.

William walks Molly along the street. The theater seems actually to be paved with stone. Each stone so heavy ten workmen couldn't lift it. He says goodbye to her at the school and goes and sits in the park. He is sitting there the entire day, staring into the water. There are figures in the water, but he cannot see them. He can only sense them. It is the same at the cemetery with all the bodies in the earth. One can feel them, but not see them. It is not that they are ghosts. It is not that impression. Simply that the centers of so many worlds rest in one another's context.

William fetches Molly from school. They return to the park. He reads to her from the newspaper. He tells her a story from his childhood. He says:

—There was a very old very rich man who said that anyone who could do what he had done would earn his entire fortune.

*What did the person have to do?

—The bet was for children only. The child would have to run away from home, leave for a distant city, make it there alive, free all the animals from the zoo, evade pursuit, and return to its home. That was the first of the tasks. There were eight in all.

*Which was the hardest one?

—Learn to actually sleep with one eye open.

*And actually be seeing from the eye, or . . . ?

—Well, otherwise it's worthless.

*I see. Did anyone actually do it?

—I think one kid got seven of them done. But he was grown up by then, so he forfeited the prize.

*Is the contest still open?

—I would imagine so. But don't run away, now. You're much too young. Just practice the sleeping with one eye open. If you can get that one, the others should follow.

Molly stands up.

*Shall we?

—Yes, let's.

They thread a path in a homeward direction, he murmuring, she gesturing, he peering at her hands in the dim evening.

There are puppets running wildly across the stage dressed as mimes. They are shot to death by other puppets who stand over them shooting and shooting down and a great ring of smoke billows out into the audience.

Molly and William are on the other side of the stage, standing very still.

The smoke billows out. When it draws back, the stage is empty once more but for William and Molly.

Molly tugs on William's sleeve.

*Do you think that the world can be saved?

—The world saved?

William smiles.

—From what?

*Those people. That, and, and Mother dying.

—That is part of our world, and can't be changed. I don't know that I would want to live in a world where things had become better, but your mother was gone. She always dreamed about that place, and I don't think I could go there without her.

Molly looks at her feet. Then she looks out into the audience. She appears to be looking right at them, one by one.

William draws in a deep breath. He continues.

—But, for you, I want it to change. One day you will be the only one of us three remaining, and then the world that includes us will be inside of you and nowhere else.

It is getting late in the evening. William tells Molly that he has to leave the house. He can't really explain why. She tries to get him to, but he won't. He has put on clothes that he rarely wears, clothes he used to wear. He looks extremely nervous. All this worries Molly immensely.

*But isn't it dangerous? We never go out this late. Oh, don't go. Don't go.

—You mustn't worry. I am the last of the great musicians.

(Does a flourish before the audience and bows.)

—All the rest have died. The government knows that. They can't harm or kill me. It would mean the end for them. Although I have not performed now in years, people know me and what I stand for. Overnight, the people would rise up. Were I to die, the revolution would rise like a second sun and everything would be burned away. The police would never take me. They know what would happen. They're too afraid. That's why they didn't kill us when they, when they killed your mother.

Molly blinks and holds the side of her dress very tight. She has always known how important her family is.

Nonetheless, she feels very proud right then and stands extremely straight.

*I am still worried, she says with her hands.

She follows him to the door. He opens it. Deep in the theater, through the door, the hallway can be seen and a door beyond. William is standing in front of that door and knocking. The wind blows the curtain of the room that Molly is standing in. She feels that she can hear a record player and a single violin, although she herself has never heard a violin, has never even seen a record player.

Now the stage is the hallway, and the door is opening. Molly comes onto the stage, beside her father. Her tail is twitching back and forth. She looks extremely small. Her father puts his arm around her. Mrs. Gibbons is on the other side of the door. Mrs. Gibbons welcomes Molly into her home. Mr. Gibbons is there also. They are an extremely kind old couple. Anyone can see that. Their house is warm and comfortable in a way that is impossible these days. It is a holdover from another time and when it disappears, even the knowledge of it will be gone.

Mrs. Gibbons is speaking to William:

—I will do this for you, said Mrs. Gibbons. You are a good father and I will do this for you and your daughter because she is very wonderful, a very wonderful young woman and I am always glad to have her here. There is always a place here in the house for a wonderful young woman who goes around with the name of Molly. But you must be careful, Mr. Drysdale, if you are going out at night, because I will tell you that Mr. Gibbons, who has just come home now this very moment, he told me that he saw a man dead not four streets over, and right in a crowd. So, you have a care.

—Is that really how I speak? Mrs. Gibbons asks Molly.

They are still beside each other in the first row.

Molly nods.

Onstage, the mouse stamps her foot.

*Be careful, she says to her father.

—Here is a key, says William, so you can put her to bed.

Mrs. Gibbons nods and closes the door. William is on the other side. He is now gone from the room. His footsteps can be heard and then they cannot.

Now Mr. Gibbons is welcoming Molly deeper into the apartment. He shows her the puppet theater, which is reproduced exactly, and is fully functional. He shows her all his materials, all his tools. He explains to her the rules of puppetry. They sit together plotting. Mrs. Gibbons brings a tray of food, which Molly devours.

In the room, Mrs. Gibbons has fallen asleep again. Molly is watching the stage desperately.

The play is drawing to a close. The little mouse is furiously writing. She is composing the play even as it occurs. Mr. Gibbons, bowed down with old feathers, is altering the puppets, is drawing the faces. He is painting the scenery. Everything is being prepared backwards, as his plan makes clear.

Mrs. Gibbons appears through a door. She sets the chairs in order. Molly is oblivious, writing at furious speed. One by one Mrs. Gibbons brings in the life-size puppets and sets them on the chairs. She dims the light. The last page of text goes to Mr. Gibbons, who settles himself behind the theater. Molly looks around. She takes a deep breath.

A LADDER OF RAIN AND THE ROOF BEYOND

And the play begins. But Molly is too worried about her father to pay attention. Her tail curls uncomfortably about her chair. Her ears twitch. She stands up and sits down. She notes the light growing in the cracks of the windows. She feels the puppets are mocking her. It is all confusing and she can't keep anything straight. Where is her father? Why isn't he back?

Finally it is too much. She jumps up and runs out of the room. She leaves the apartment, running down the stairs out into the street. It is early morning and the light is very bright. The stone buildings are so actual that they hurt her. The trees don't move. Everything is in her way. She runs through the trees and through the streets, searching for anything, any clue. Where is he? Where has he gone?

She makes her way down a long boulevard, and an old woman, out early with a broom, calls to her. She runs on instead.

A young man sees her from a window. He calls to her, too.

Down the boulevard she goes, and reaches the lake. There in the park, a paper is fluttering. She grabs at it. She gets it in her hands. It is the work of the conspirators, the plotters, even she can tell that, hand-pressed on contraband machines. She snatches at it even as she holds it and tries to read the faintly pressed letters.

THE VIOLINIST WILLIAM DRYSDALE HAS BEEN FOULLY MURDERED IN THE STREET BY THE FORCES OF THE GOVERNMENT ++

She falls to the ground. She is clutching at the sheet. She doesn't know what to do with it. Can she not see him? Not even once? Has it happened? Is she alone?

*He is dead. He is dead.

All around her there is singing in the streets. That's what it sounded like, like singing, but it is the playing of a violin. The sound rises up and trembles the buildings, runs through the streets. It reaches her and sweeps her along with it. It is all over. There is nothing left.

Her hands were on her coat, they were shaking and tugging. Her face was in them and then out. She saw the street and the rutted gardens, the rows of houses, the rising light. She was shouting and she was by the ground. Her hands were on it. Through the trees she could see the lake and upon it, all as before, always as before.

And the mouse took her own life.

The veiled jester comes out onto the stage. Everyone in the room is asleep.

—Molly, he says. Molly.

He is holding a long bone, and there are directions carved into its length.

FIN

HERE ACKNOWLEDGE:

Thordis, Alda, Nora, Nutmeg, Salazar Larus, Nun, Klara.

Jenny Jackson, Kate Runde, & all at Vintage.

Billy Kingsland, David Kuhn, & Kuhn Projects.